BREED LOVE

LOVE IN THE FAMILY

Charles Gober

ISBN: 979-8-89525-904-7

Dedication

This book is dedicated to everyone who has supported me in my book-writing endeavors.

About the Author

Charles Gober was born in Michigan and is a US Navy veteran. Writing has always been a passion of his, and with 'The Love in the Family,' his dream of becoming a published author has finally come to fruition.

He hopes and wishes that the readers will look forward to and enjoy his upcoming books.

Preface

Welcome to a story where destinies intertwine through moments of fate, redemption, and the enduring bonds that shape our lives. It's a narrative that follows the lives of Susan and Vance, two individuals deeply affected by past traumas and their pursuit of justice.

Susan's journey begins with a tragic assault during her youth, a pivotal event that influences her resilience in facing life's challenges. We witness her navigating the complexities of family dynamics, friendships, and the lasting impact of her trauma. Her story highlights the strength found in confronting brutal truths and the power of resilience.

Vance's path initially seems separate but gradually converges with Susan's, driven by shared experiences and hidden connections. His life is defined by loyalty, responsibility, and the weight of buried secrets. From unexpected relationships with Hattie and later Susan, Vance's journey unfolds with themes of love, loss, and the search for personal truth.

As their stories intersect, we delve into themes of forgiveness, betrayal, and the profound effects of past traumas on their lives. Each chapter reveals more about their intertwined destinies, uncovering complex relationships and the enduring quest for justice and redemption.

This narrative goes beyond individual tales; it reflects the universal human experience—how we endure hardships, seek healing, and find meaning in our connections with others. Join us on a journey through the lives of Susan, Vasnce, and those around them as their paths collide in unexpected and poignant ways.

Contents

Chapter 1

In a small town nestled between rolling hills and sprawling fields, Susan found herself trapped in the daily grind of life. Every morning, she embarked on a journey that began with a weary sigh and ended with an exhausted slump. Susan was a waitress at the only truck stop in town, a place where the transient hum of highway traffic blended with the chatter of locals seeking refuge from the monotony of rural life.

The truck stop was a dusty haven for travelers, a pit stop on their way to destinations unknown. For Susan, however, it was the epicenter of her world – a place that demanded her attention and resilience every day. The establishment was situated thirty minutes away from her modest home, a distance that seemed to grow longer with every passing day.

A normal day in Susan's life began long before the first rays of sunlight kissed the sleepy town awake. She relied on unreliable local transport, a bus that creaked and groaned through narrow roads and winding paths. On a good day, the journey took a solid hour, leaving her feeling more drained before her shift started.

The truck stop itself was a curious amalgamation of stories. Conversations of travelers from distant lands mingled with the tales of locals who found solace in its worn-out booths.

Susan moved through the tables with a practiced grace, her worn-out notepad in hand, ready to take orders with a smile that concealed the fatigue etched into her features.

Being a waitress was not exactly a ticket to societal respect. The townsfolk, with their conservative values and judgments, often regarded her role as less than honorable. The arduous hours and meager pay seemed to be the unspoken price for choosing a path deemed unworthy by the community. However, Susan persevered, driven by a silent determination that burned within her.

Harassment had become an unwelcome companion on her journey. For Susan, it was like facing a storm every Tuesday – relentless, unforgiving, and always looming on the horizon. The truck stop, with its transient clientele, became a breeding ground for inappropriate remarks and lingering gazes. Susan bore the weight of their scrutiny with a stoic facade, refusing to let their disdain chip away at her resolve.

Yet, amidst the chaos of clinking cutlery and the persistent drone of conversation, Susan found solace in small moments. The worn-out jukebox played familiar tunes that carried her away, if only for a fleeting moment, from the relentless demands of her job. There were occasional glimpses of kindness from strangers, a sympathetic smile, or a generous tip that briefly illuminated the shadows of her daily struggles.

Fate, it seemed, had a way of intertwining destinies, and in Susan's case, it happened at the very place she considered both her sanctuary and battleground: the truck stop.

John, a rugged and earnest young man, entered Susan's world on an ordinary afternoon. His eyes met hers across the bustling diner, and a connection sparked between them. What started as a casual conversation unfolded into something profound. Their laughter resonated amidst the clinks of cutlery, and the truck stop's din became a backdrop to the blossoming of a tender love.

As the weeks passed, Susan and John found themselves drawn to each other in ways that defied explanation. Shared dreams, whispered confessions, and stolen glances wove the fabric of their connection. Still grappling with the echoes of her past struggles, Susan found solace in John's unwavering support and genuine affection.

Their love story unfolded with an undeniable swiftness. Before either of them fully comprehended the depth of their feelings, Susan and John stood at the precipice of a life-altering decision. At the tender age of 18, Susan made the daring choice to marry the man who had become the anchor in her turbulent existence. The truck stop, witness to countless stories, now bore witness to the union of two souls navigating the unpredictable journey of life together.

The small ceremony, held amidst the rustic charm, marked the beginning of Susan and John's shared adventure. Despite the skepticism that lingered in the judgmental gazes of the townsfolk, the young couple embarked on their journey hand in hand. The truck stop, a silent spectator to their love story, continued to serve as the backdrop to their evolving lives.

Marriage brought its own set of challenges, but Susan and John faced them with a resilience born out of love. The truck stop, once a symbol of Susan's struggle, now became a place where the couple shared meals, exchanged stories, and weathered the storms of life together. Amid the hustle and bustle, Susan discovered a sanctuary within the walls of the diner

– a place where the echoes of her past hardships were drowned out by the laughter and camaraderie she found in John's company.

Before the whirlwind of love and marriage swept her away, Susan's life was anchored in the modest home she shared with Hattie and Earl, her middle-aged biological parents. Their lives were a delicate balance, teetering on the edge of financial strain. It wasn't a tumultuous existence, but the weight of responsibility hung in the air, making every day a quiet struggle to make ends meet.

With her worn hands and a heart weathered by life's challenges, Hattie worked tirelessly to keep the household afloat. Earl, a man of few words but endless determination, contributed what he could to support the family. Together, they formed a unit bound by love and a shared commitment to weathering life's storms.

Their humble dwelling bore the marks of a family navigating the complexities of survival. Susan, even in her youth, shouldered responsibilities beyond her years. Despite the challenges, Susan found solace in the warmth of familial bonds. Evenings were spent gathered around a modest dinner table, where laughter and love served as the currency that fortified their connection. The truck stop, where Susan had found employment, became a beacon of hope and opportunity amid their financial struggles.

In the tight-knit neighborhood, Susan discovered a sense of community that extended beyond the confines of her home. Friends became extended family, and their doors were always open to shared stories and moments of respite from life's hardships. Susan, with her infectious spirit, often sought refuge in the company of these friends, creating a mosaic of memories that painted the canvas of her youth.

The neighborhood, with its quaint houses and familiar faces, became a sanctuary for Susan. In the company of friends, she found an escape from the weight of responsibility that pressed upon her at home. Together, they navigated the landscape of adolescence, sharing dreams, secrets, and the simple joys that formed their youth.

It was in these moments, away from the demanding roles of daughter and provider, that Susan discovered the beauty of friendship and the power of shared experiences. Once a place of employment, the truck stop transformed into a meeting point for laughter and stories, a bridge connecting Susan's familial responsibilities with the refuge of friendship.

Eventually, John and Susan moved, and he took her under her wing. But she still missed the embrace of her diverse relationships – be it the enduring love of her husband or the comforting camaraderie of her friends in the neighborhood – Susan discovered the strength to face life's challenges head-on. The truck stop, once a symbol of struggle, transformed into a place where the echoes of her journey reverberated alongside the laughter and shared moments that defined her existence. And so, as Susan continued to navigate the complexities of life, the lessons learned from her roots and the unexpected connections along the way became the guiding lights on her journey.

However, the echoes of Susan's resilient journey were shadowed by a night that left an indelible mark on her past. It was a chilling evening when Susan, at the tender age of 13, was walking home from her friend's house. Once a haven of familiarity and comfort, the neighborhood transformed into an eerie labyrinth as the shadows stretched across the quiet streets.

As she traversed the familiar path, the air thickened with unsettling tension. A masked man emerged from the darkness, a sinister figure with malevolent intentions. Susan's heart quickened as fear gripped her like a vice. The ordinary walk home, a routine she had gotten used to, transformed into a nightmare that would haunt her for years to come.

A masked man, an ominous presence in the obsidian night, moved with a predatory intent. He cornered Susan, shattering the innocence of her adolescence with a cruel twist of fate. The night became a canvas of horror as he attempted something heinous and unimaginable, threatening to steal away the light that had illuminated Susan's life.

In that harrowing moment, Susan summoned a strength she didn't know she possessed. A primal survival instinct surged within her, and she fought back against the masked assailant with every ounce of her being. The struggle between vulnerability and resilience played out in the silent streets as Susan fought to reclaim control over her narrative. However, it was all for naught. Susan was caught in the hands of the predator. She screamed and screeched in agony as the man forced himself on her.

The episode that had unfolded in the shadows of that night took an unexpected turn when the police arrived. Susan found herself caught in a whirlwind of emotions as the masked man narrowly escaped the police. Neighbors, drawn by the commotion, rushed to the scene, their voices forming a chorus of defiance against the darkness that had descended upon their quiet and peaceful community. The traumatic event cast a long, haunting shadow over Susan's life. The truck stop, her familial home, and the neighborhood that once offered solace now bore witness to the invisible scars that marked her spirit. The aftermath of that fateful night tested the limits of Susan's resilience, leaving her grappling with the trauma that threatened to define her existence.

In the aftermath, the legal system got to work, its gears grinding to deliver justice. However, in an era where DNA technology was not readily available, the tools for a comprehensive investigation were limited. Susan, scarred both physically and emotionally, faced the harsh reality that the assailant's identity might remain a haunting mystery.

The absence of advanced forensic technology meant that the scars on Susan's body and the trauma etched into her memory would be the only evidence of the nightmarish encounter. The inability to perform further tests cast a shadow of uncertainty over the pursuit of justice, leaving Susan to grapple with the knowledge that closure might remain elusive.

The lack of concrete evidence did not diminish the resilience that Susan displayed in the face of adversity. The truck stop, which had witnessed both her struggles and moments of triumph, became a sanctuary where she found solace amidst the echoes of the past. Her family and friends rallied around her, offering unwavering support as she navigated the complex terrain of healing. However, just as she thought her suffering was over and that the path forward would only be that of recovery, she found out she was pregnant.

Chapter 2

Susan's journey to motherhood was a tumultuous one, marked by the daunting question of who the father was. One night, having woken up by the agonizing pain of contractions, Susan called for her parents, who then took her to the hospital to give birth, a moment that should have been filled with joy and excitement. Little did she know that this was not going to be the end of her troubles.

As Susan arrived at the hospital, her anticipation was mixed with anxiety. The months leading up to this day had been filled with the usual blend of joy and apprehension that accompanies pregnancy. However, what awaited her at the hospital was far from the typical birthing experience.

Unexpected complications marred Susan's pregnancy, casting a shadow over the anticipated joy of impending motherhood. The medical team, acutely aware of the gravity of the situation, swiftly responded by administering a sedative. This decision aimed not only to alleviate the complications but also to secure a safe delivery for both Susan and her unborn child. In the face of uncertainty, the medical professionals worked diligently to navigate the complexities of the situation, prioritizing the well-being of both mother and baby.

The sedative served as a strategic intervention, a necessary step to mitigate risks and pave the way for a successful and safe birthing process. The hushed urgency of the medical team underscored the delicate balance they sought to achieve, ensuring that Susan's journey through childbirth would ultimately culminate in the arrival of a healthy and thriving newborn.

The sedative served its purpose by rendering Susan unconscious, shielding her from the intricate and potentially distressing medical procedures that lay ahead. As she drifted into a state of temporary oblivion, the medical team worked diligently to navigate the complexities of her pregnancy and provide the necessary care for a successful delivery.

Amid the challenges and uncertainties, Susan's body labored to bring forth life. When she awoke, she found herself on the other side of consciousness, the air filled with a mixture of relief and tension. The medical staff shared both concern and relief as the situation was delicate and the outcome uncertain.

In the midst of this rollercoaster, Susan met her newborn son, Vance. The joy that should have accompanied this moment was overshadowed by the trauma she had endured. Vance, a symbol of hope and new beginnings, became a bittersweet reminder of the pain she had faced during childbirth.

The scars Susan carried weren't just physical; they ran deep into the emotional and psychological realms. The non-consensual nature of the medical interventions left her grappling with a sense of violation and powerlessness. The birthing process, which ideally fosters a sense of empowerment and connection with one's body, had been tainted by circumstances beyond her control.

As Susan anxiously waited for news on her son's well-being, a disconcerting turn of events unfolded. Vance, still in the delicate early stages of life, had been transferred to the hospital nursery for further monitoring and care. It was there that an inadvertent mistake occurred, one that would add another layer of complexity to Susan's already challenging journey.

In a few days' time, Vance's condition stabilized, and he was allowed to be taken back home. Susan, relieved to finally be out of the hospital, quickly began packing and, along with her newborn, headed home. However, as the days passed, Susan began to sense a disconnection with her child. Her maternal instincts picked up on subtle cues, and an underlying unease settled in, but she always brushed it off, deeming it as a product of exhaustion and sleepless nights. Little did she know that her maternal instincts weren't a false alarm and that something life-altering had happened at the hospital.

In the confines of the same hospital, a jubilant atmosphere enveloped the room as Sharon and Brian Breedlove joyously celebrated the arrival of their newborn, John. The radiant couple, Sharon and Brian, had embarked on the journey of matrimony a mere year ago, forging a union that radiated love and contentment. Eager to embrace parenthood, they wasted no time in welcoming a new life into their midst.

The newlyweds, Sharon and Brian, shared a blissful life marked by shared dreams and aspirations. Driven by their deep connection and a shared desire for a family, they decided to embark on the transformative journey of parenthood at the earliest opportunity.

The momentous day arrived when Sharon, the proud mother, cradled her newborn son, John, affectionately known as Eddie. Overwhelmed with joy, Sharon's eyes sparkled with happiness as she held the precious bundle of joy in her arms. Her maternal instincts kicked in, and she embraced the responsibility with utmost care, ensuring that John's introduction to the world was filled with warmth and tenderness.

As Sharon gazed down at little John, the embodiment of their love, a profound sense of fulfillment washed over her. The room resonated with the harmonious blend of parental joy and the promising essence of a new life. The love that bound Brian and Sharon had now expanded to include their precious son, creating a familial tapestry woven with love, commitment, and anticipation for the future.

The significance of this moment extended beyond the hospital room, symbolizing the continuity of life and the enduring cycle of love and family. For Sharon and Brian, this was not just the birth of a child; it was the moment their shared dreams had been realized and marked the beginning of a new chapter in their lives.

Several months into caring for her child, a disheartening realization began to dawn upon her – a poignant awareness that her connection with the little one seemed elusive. Despite the tender moments of caregiving, a somber truth unfolded: the child displayed signs of detachment. Persistent cries and frequent tantrums marked the child's behavior, creating a palpable distance between them. Navigating through the intricacies of motherhood, Sharon found herself grappling with a profound sense of disconnection.

The child's incessant cries became a poignant soundtrack to her days, echoing the struggle within their relationship. Each wail seemed to underscore the widening gap, a silent plea for understanding that remained unanswered. The child's finicky nature added another layer of complexity as every attempt to nurture and comfort him was met with resistance. Sharon, caught in the vortex of these challenges, felt the tendrils of emotional separation encircle her.

The sense of drifting away became an emotional undertow, pulling at the core of her maternal identity. As she navigated the turbulent waters of parenthood, doubts and insecurities loomed like storm clouds on the horizon. The child, once an extension of herself, now appeared like a distant entity shrouded in a veil of mystery. In those moments of solitude, she grappled with the disconcerting notion that the child might not truly be her own.

The echoes of this disconnection reverberated in the silent moments when the child's room was filled only with the sound of discontent. As she tried to decipher the child's needs, a pervasive sense of inadequacy lingered. The mother-child bond, which she had envisioned as an unbreakable thread weaving their lives together, now seemed fragile and tenuous.

Yet, amidst the shadows of uncertainty, there remained a flicker of hope. The mother's heart, resilient and steadfast, yearned to bridge the gap and reclaim the sense of kinship that seemed to slip away. She embarked on a journey of introspection, seeking to understand the web of emotions that defined their relationship. In this crucible of maternal love, she resolved to forge a connection, one that transcended the challenges and spoke to the essence of motherhood.

Susan, on the other hand, was dealing with the same issues; however, she continued to attend to her child. Unbeknownst to the two mothers, in the nursery of the hospital where their newborns rested in clear cribs, each identified by a name tag, Vance's identification had been entangled with another newborn, John. The mix-up seemed inconsequential at first, a simple oversight in the flurry of activity within the hospital. However, this unintentional error would set the stage for a series of events that would unravel in the days to come.

The switch went unnoticed initially, and Susan and Sharon, still recovering from the physical and emotional toll of childbirth, were left unaware of the mistake. Vance, now bearing the name tag intended for John or Eddie, continued to receive care under this new identity. Meanwhile, John, unaware of the mix-up, was attended to as if he were Susan's biological child.

Hence, all this time, Susan had been raising Eddie, who she believed to be Vance. Simultaneously, Sharon, who lovingly cradled the infant she presumed to be her biological son, Eddie, was unknowingly nurturing Vance. The switch in name tags had woven a complex tapestry of mistaken identities, blurring the lines of familial connection for both unsuspecting mothers.

Amidst the tumultuous events that had unfolded, an ominous undercurrent lingered in the shadows of Brian Breedlove's character—something Sharon, in her one year of marriage, had been too trusting to discern. Little did she know, there was a sinister dimension to Brian's actions that eluded her understanding. Throughout their brief union, Brian exhibited peculiar behavior, frequently departing their home without explanation and returning with an unsettling air about him.

Initially, Sharon attributed this to a potential struggle with an uncontrolled drinking problem, but the truth lurking beneath Brian's facade was far more malevolent than she could fathom.

Brian Breedlove was a man shrouded in layers of secrecy, concealing dark truths that would cast an ominous shadow over the lives of both Sharon and Susan. The unraveling of his enigmatic nature heralded a harrowing turn in the narrative as the depths of Brian's transgressions began to surface.

Sharon, with her innate trust and perhaps a touch of naivety, had not suspected the magnitude of Brian's capacity for deception. The moments of his unexplained absences and peculiar conduct were fragments of a more profound mystery that she had yet to unravel. Behind the veneer of marital bliss, Brian harbored secrets that were not only deeply disturbing but also posed a threat to the foundations of their lives.

The initial suspicion of an unchecked drinking problem paled in comparison to the gravity of Brian's actions. His secret activities were a testament to a more sinister aspect of his character, one that Sharon had not anticipated. The unraveling of this disconcerting truth marked a pivotal juncture in their relationship as the façade of normalcy crumbled, revealing the unsettling reality that lay underneath.

As the web of Brian's deceit began to tighten, the repercussions extended beyond Sharon to Susan, linking the lives of the two unsuspecting women in a disturbing twist of fate. The gravity of Brian's heinous secrets now cast a dark shadow over both households, entwining their destinies in a way that neither Sharon nor Susan could have foreseen.

In this labyrinth of deception, Sharon found herself at a crossroads, grappling with the revelation that the man she had vowed to spend her life with was concealing a malevolence that defied comprehension. The sinister undertones of Brian's actions were not just a personal betrayal but a catalyst for a more ominous chapter in their life that awaited them.

The narrative, once shaped by the seemingly idyllic union of Sharon and Brian, now took an unexpected turn, propelling both women into a maelstrom of uncertainty and fear. The secrets that Brian harbored were like poison seeping into the very core of their lives, leaving a trail of devastation in their wake. As Sharon and Susan stood on the precipice of this unsettling revelation, the true extent of Brian's malevolence was yet to fully unfold, casting a long and foreboding shadow over the entwined destinies of these unsuspecting women.

Chapter 3

John Smith, the patriarch of the Smith family, and Brian Breedlove, the head of the Breedlove clan, resided in different neighborhoods with their respective families.

Happiness radiated in the dwelling John's family resided in. Their family comprised himself, his wife Susan, their son Vance (Eddie), and Jennifer, whom John had welcomed into their familial embrace through adoption when Vance (Eddie) was four years old. The Smith home echoed with laughter and warmth, largely attributed to John's humor and wisdom, which seamlessly connected the two families. Meanwhile, Susan, with her boundless warmth and love, served as the glue, forging strong emotional ties between family members. She bestowed upon Vance (Eddie) and Jennifer a profound sense of being cherished, making them feel like the center of the universe.

In the Breedlove residence, Brian and Sharon exemplified the same love and dedication seen in the Smith family. Their unwavering affection towards their son, Eddie (Vance), was evident in their prompt and attentive care. Within the Breedlove household, Brian and Sharon demonstrated a love and commitment akin to that observed in the Smith family. Their attentive and immediate care for their son, Eddie (Vance), underscored the depth of their affection.

Unbeknownst to the two families, Vance (Eddie) and Eddie (Vance) attended the same school throughout much of their lives; however, a captivating twist of fate prevented them from acknowledging each other's existence until high school.

***

After meeting at a truck stop where Susan was dedicatedly working as a waitress, John and Susan embarked on a significant journey together. Their initial encounter evolved into a lifelong connection, leading to marriage. Their love story, encapsulated in Vance (Eddie), became a foundational narrative that instilled a profound sense of destiny in both.

Back in school, with Eddie (Vance) and Vance (Eddie) having taken up quite a few similar classes, it was inevitable that their lives would take a new direction. After being paired for a physics project, their friendship flourished beyond the confines of the classroom, with the inseparable companions opting to share lunch, spend after-school hours together, and participate in sports that reinforced the strength of their bond.

The parallel lives of the Smiths and the Breedloves, once running in separate lanes, began to converge as a result of the camaraderie between Vance and Eddie. The symphony of their interconnected lives played on, creating a harmonious melody that echoed through the city streets they called home.

One day, after Vance (Eddie)'s class, his excitement bubbled up as he spotted the wrestling tryouts flyer in the hallway. He and Eddie(Vance) had been talking about it during their lunch breaks. So, being the most responsible friend he was, he immediately dialed Eddie (Vance)'s number.

"Hey, Eddie! Have you seen the wrestling tryout flyer? This is our chance!" Vance (Eddie) spoke enthusiastically,

"Wrestling tryouts? Count me in, man! This is going to be awesome! You know I can't say no to that."

Vance (Eddie) laughed, "Absolutely, Eddie! We've talked about hitting the mats together someday, and now's the perfect opportunity. Let's show them what we're made of!"

"You bet, Vance (Eddie)! We'll be the dynamic duo of the wrestling world. Can't wait to hit those mats with you!" Eddie was determined.

"That's the plan, bud. Get ready for some serious tag-team action. See you at tryouts!"

"You got it! Let's make our mark on that wrestling mat!"

That conversation shaped the pivotal chapter in the lives of Vance (Eddie) and Eddie (Vance) as it took center stage—their joint leadership of the school's wrestling team. Both young men, with a shared passion for the sport, emerged as formidable leaders on the mat. Their complementary skills and camaraderie translated into an effective partnership that not only bolstered the team's performance but also strengthened the bond between the two boys.

The wrestling team became a ground on which Vance (Eddie) and Eddie (Vance) had a chance to display their shared determination, discipline, and mutual respect for the sport. Leading their peers with a blend of strategy and sportsmanship, the duo left an indelible mark on the school's athletic legacy. The wrestling mat transformed into a stage where the interconnected destinies of the Smith and Breedlove families were played out.

***

Amidst the fervor of wrestling matches and the shared triumphs over math, a new chapter emerged; life took an unexpected turn when Eddie found himself drawn to the magnetic personality of Jennifer, Vance's (Eddie's) sister. Their connection went beyond the confines of familial ties, evolving into a romantic relationship that added a layer of complexity to the intertwined destinies of the two families.

The blossoming romance between Eddie and Jennifer was not without its challenges. Negotiating the delicate terrain of dating a friend's sibling required tact and sensitivity. Vance (Eddie), being the protective brother, initially harbored reservations about Eddie dating his sister. However, as he witnessed the genuine love and respect Eddie demonstrated towards Jennifer, his concerns gradually transformed into acceptance.

On the other hand, the dynamics of the friendships between Eddie and Vance underwent a remarkable shift as they assumed leadership positions within the wrestling team. Vance (Eddie), with his commanding and powerful approach, seamlessly complemented Eddie's strategic acumen, creating a synergy that set them apart. Their individual strengths converged to form an unstoppable force, leaving an indelible mark on the team and the school community at large.

Vance (Eddie)'s wrestling style was marked by an unyielding determination and physical prowess that struck fear into the hearts of opponents. His powerful approach wasn't just about raw strength but also a manifestation of relentless discipline and a tenacious spirit. Vance (Eddie) became a symbol of unwavering commitment on the mat, inspiring not only his teammates but also earning the respect of rivals.

On the other hand, Eddie (Vance) brought a different dimension to their formidable partnership. His strategic thinking and calculated approach to wrestling added finesse to Vance (Eddie)'s power. Eddie (Vance)'s ability to analyze opponents, anticipate moves, and formulate effective strategies turned their wrestling duo into a well-rounded force. It wasn't just about overpowering opponents; it was about outsmarting them on the mat.

Together, Vance and Eddie were a dynamic duo, seamlessly blending brawn and brains. Their leadership roles extended beyond the wrestling mat, influencing the team's ethos and camaraderie. They became mentors to their teammates, fostering an environment of mutual support and shared success. The wrestling team, once a collection of individuals, transformed into a cohesive unit under their guidance.

The impact of Vance and Eddie's partnership extended beyond the confines of the wrestling arena. Their influence rippled through the school, shaping perceptions of teamwork, dedication, and excellence. The duo became emblematic of the school's wrestling legacy, with their image synonymous with triumph and resilience.

In essence, Vance and Eddie's journey from friends to leaders on the wrestling team encapsulated the transformative power of collaboration, showcasing how the convergence of individual strengths could create an unstoppable force. Their legacy in the school was not merely defined by victories on the mat but by the enduring impact of their friendship and leadership on the entire community.

***

The crescendo of the Smith and Breedlove saga reached its zenith with the high school graduation of Vance and Eddie, marking the end of one chapter and the commencement of new, uncharted territories. The ceremony itself was a culmination of years of hard work, shared triumphs, and the enduring bonds that had formed among the families.

Vance and Eddie stood side by side, adorned in graduation robes, symbolizing not just the end of their high school journey but the beginning of a new phase in their lives. The cheers of their families, intertwined in a sea of emotions, resonated through the auditorium as diplomas were handed out, signifying their accomplishments.

The graduation party that ensued was a jubilant celebration, a festive amalgamation of the two families and their shared history, which they were oblivious to. The venue echoed with laughter, music, and the clinking of glasses, serving as a backdrop to heartfelt toasts and speeches that celebrated the achievements of the graduates. As the night unfolded, it became evident that the Smiths and Breedloves were not just friends; they were a family, bonded by shared experiences and an enduring love that transcended the confines of blood.

Eddie (Vance) and Jennifer, amidst the festivities, found themselves at a juncture where their individual paths were set to diverge. The prospect of college beckoned, introducing a new chapter in their lives. However, the love that had blossomed between them in the halls of high school persisted, resilient in the face of change. The decision to continue their relationship beyond the familiar grounds of their hometown was not without its challenges.

Eddie (Vance) enrolled in a university that promised new opportunities and experiences while Jennifer embarked on her own academic journey. The physical distance between them became a test of their commitment, prompting late-night phone calls, heartfelt letters, and occasional visits that bridged the miles. The challenges of a long-distance relationship were met with resilience, and the couple discovered that their love could withstand the tests of time and space.

The graduation chapter served as a poignant transition point, highlighting the resilience of bonds forged through laughter, shared dreams, and the triumphs of high school wrestling matches. The intertwined destinies of the Smith and Breedlove families continue to evolve, each member navigating the currents of change, growth, and the inexorable passage of time.

The continuation of Eddie (Vance) and Jennifer's love story marked a conscious decision to navigate the complexities that life threw their way. Acknowledging the hurdles posed by conflicting schedules, they were realistic about the potential strains on their time and energy. However, their willingness to confront these challenges head-on reflected a deep commitment to making their relationship endure.

They recognized that sustaining a connection amid conflicting demands required patience and a concerted effort. Despite the uncertainties that lay ahead, Eddie and Jennifer were resolute in their desire to nurture and sustain their love.

The couple’s commitment shone through as their decision to give their relationship the time it needed demonstrated a mature understanding of the intricacies involved. Rather than succumbing to the potential pitfalls, they embraced the challenges, demonstrating a shared belief that their love story was worth the investment of time and patience.

Chapter 4

Vance and Eddie, close friends with dreams that diverged, stood at the crossroads of their academic futures. The duo's shared quest to find a suitable college, each harboring distinct aspirations, faced the challenge of selecting one that could accommodate their individual career goals. Vance (Eddie) had nurtured dreams of becoming a distinguished doctor, envisioning a path that would lead him to prominence in the medical field. On the other hand, Eddie (Vance) had set his sights on the realm of computer sciences with a backup plan involving his passion for wrestling. The diversity of their ambitions presented a conundrum as they navigated through a multitude of options, each seeming inadequate to fully capture their aspirations.

Vance and Eddie found themselves ensnared in the intricate web of uncertainty that shrouded their future paths. The tension between them heightened as they grappled with the challenge of reconciling their disparate dreams within the limited array of available choices. The daunting prospect of making life-altering decisions weighed heavily on their minds, casting a shadow over their future goals.

In the midst of this confusion and indecision, a beacon of hope suddenly illuminated their path. Vance and Eddie stumbled upon a college that miraculously met both of their criteria, providing an unexpected resolution to the dilemma that had clouded their thoughts. This discovery brought a sense of relief, as the chosen college not only pledged academic excellence but also boasted a conveniently ideal location. This geographical advantage offered the friends a comforting familiarity that alleviated the stress associated with venturing into the unknown.

The proximity of the college to Susan's parents, Earl and Hattie, infused an additional layer of warmth and connection into the narrative. Earl and Hattie, portrayed as affectionate sweethearts, became integral characters in the unfolding story. The narrative painted a vivid picture of their welcoming nature, as they graciously opened their hearts and home to Eddie (Vance). In doing so, they extended the bonds of friendship that Vance and Eddie had shared for the longest time by deciding to rent a place together, embedding family ties within the tapestry of their collegiate journey.

The significance of Susan's parents being nearby not only added a practical convenience but also deepened the emotional resonance of the narrative. It exemplified the idea that the chosen college was not merely a stepping stone for Vance and Eddie but a place where familial connections could be nurtured and expanded. The family's presence provided a sense of security and belonging, making the college experience more than just an academic pursuit—it became a holistic journey enriched by the warmth of relationships.

As Vance (Eddie) introduced Eddie (Vance) to Susan's parents, the genuine happiness and warmth exhibited by Earl and Hattie created a heartening atmosphere.

Vance and Eddie's journey became a poignant exploration of the transformative power of choices and the resilience of friendships in the face of diverging paths. Continuing their journey towards a shared future, Vance and Eddie engaged in a thoughtful discussion about practicalities and financial considerations. The realization dawned upon them that attending college involved not only academic pursuits but also the practicalities of living arrangements and expenses.

With a shared commitment to their dreams and a desire to ease the financial burden of college life, Vance and Eddie deliberated on the prospect of finding a suitable place to live. Renting a room together not only offered the advantage of shared expenses but also fostered an environment of mutual support and camaraderie. It became a decision rooted in practicality and a testament to the strength of their friendship.

As they scoured the local housing options, the friends sought a residence that not only fit within their budget constraints but also provided a conducive environment for their academic pursuits. The process of selecting the right accommodation became a collaborative effort, reflecting their shared commitment to creating a conducive and supportive living space.

The nuances of their shared living experience – the laughter, the challenges, and the growth that comes with navigating the responsibilities of independence.

The decision to rent a room together marked the commencement of a transformative phase in Vance and Eddie's college journey. The shared living experience became an intricate tapestry woven with laughter, challenges, and profound personal growth as they navigated the responsibilities of independence. The room, initially chosen out of practicality, swiftly evolved into a cornerstone of their college narrative, shaping the very essence of their friendships and exerting a substantial influence on the trajectory of their individual journeys.

Laughter became a constant companion within the walls of their shared space. Late-night conversations, impromptu wrestling matches, and shared jokes filled the room with a sense of camaraderie and joy. It was in these moments of shared mirth that their friendship transcended the practical considerations of cohabitation, deepening into a genuine connection. The laughter, echoing through the room, served as a constant reminder of the bonds they had formed and the sanctuary they had created amidst the challenges of college life.

Yet, shared living wasn't devoid of challenges. The room bore witness to disagreements, from trivial matters like household chores to more significant issues that tested the resilience of their friendship. These challenges, however, became catalysts for growth. Through communication and compromise, Vance and Eddie learned to navigate the complexities of living together, emerging not only as friends but as individuals who understood the importance of adapting and accommodating each other's differences.

For Vance and Eddie, college had evolved into a shared mission to not only navigate the challenges of daily life but also to alleviate the financial strain of their education. Recognizing the importance of taking charge of their financial responsibilities, the duo saw college as a springboard for a joint endeavor toward employment.

The idea of seeking employment within the town presented itself as a pragmatic solution, a tangible means to address the financial challenges associated with their education. This decision reflected their determination to proactively manage their financial responsibilities and, in the process, enhance the overall quality of their college experience. It wasn't just about attending classes; it was about embracing the responsibilities that came with adulthood and actively contributing to their own educational journey.

The prospect of finding jobs within the town became a practical manifestation of their commitment to self-sufficiency. Rather than relying solely on academic pursuits, Vance and Eddie recognized the value of gaining real-world experience through employment. This approach not only offered a financial reprieve but also enriched their college experience by providing insights and skills that transcended the confines of the classroom.

In making the decision to seek employment, Vance and Eddie demonstrated a proactive approach to their financial well-being, turning their college experience into a multifaceted journey. Their joint endeavor to secure jobs within the town showcased a blend of determination, responsibility, and a pragmatic outlook on the challenges that accompany higher education.

The friends understood that employment wasn't merely a means to cover tuition and living expenses but also a gateway to real-world experiences that could complement their academic pursuits. This perspective infused their job search with a sense of purpose beyond financial gain, transforming it into a quest for personal and professional growth.

The town, with its local businesses and community establishments, became the stage for Vance and Eddie's endeavors. Their exploration ranged from part-time positions in cafes and retail stores to internships carefully aligned with their career aspirations. This diverse approach not only broadened their skill sets but also allowed them to make meaningful connections within the local community, expanding their sense of belonging beyond the walls of academia.

Through the shared job searches, Vance and Eddie not only achieved financial stability but also deepened their bond as friends. The highs and lows of the job market became shared experiences, fostering a camaraderie that transcended the professional sphere. In the face of challenges, they offered each other unwavering support, providing encouragement and sharing insights gained from their individual journeys.

Their collective experiences in the workplace didn't just contribute to their financial well-being; they became integral parts of their college narrative. The memories and anecdotes forged during their employment adventures enriched their overall college experience, turning mundane tasks into stories that would be recounted with fondness in years to come.

Chapter 5

It was a Saturday morning, and Eddie (Vance) decided to surprise Jennifer on her day off. The sun had painted the sky with hues of pink and orange as he knocked on her front door. Jennifer, still in high school with two years left to graduate, opened the door with a surprised yet delighted smile.

"Eddie! What brings you here?" she exclaimed.

"Just thought I'd drop by and spend the day with you," Eddie (Vance) replied with a grin and went in for a hug. “I’ve missed you,” he whispered in her ear.

The morning unfolded with the promise of adventures as Eddie (Vance) and Jennifer embarked on a journey through the heart of their town, the streets becoming the canvas for their shared escapade. The sun, a benevolent witness, bestowed warmth upon their day as they meandered through hidden alleys and familiar corners. Eddie (Vance), captivated by the vivacity that emanated from Jennifer, found himself marveling at the kaleidoscope of emotions reflected in her sparkling eyes.

As the day unfolded, they found themselves drawn to the tranquility of a local park, a verdant haven nestled within the bustling town. The rustling leaves overhead played a symphony of whispers, setting them up for a moment of shared serenity beneath the canopy of a sprawling oak tree. The air was alive with the shared laughter that echoed between them, a melody of connection.

In the midst of their idyllic day, the rhythm of their laughter was interrupted by the familiar buzz of Jennifer's phone. Apologizing with a sheepish smile, she excused herself, leaving Eddie (Vance) alone with the rustling leaves and the distant symphony of children's laughter.

Curiosity, a relentless companion, nudged Eddie to glance at Jennifer's phone. The screen illuminated with calls and texts from a certain Mike, casting shadows of doubt across the canvas of their carefree day. Concern mingled with confusion, creating a storm of emotions within Eddie's mind. He grappled with the moral dilemma of invading her privacy against the undeniable need for an explanation.

As Eddie (Vance) deliberated, the sunlight filtered through the leaves above, casting a dappled pattern on the ground beneath. The park, once a sanctuary of shared laughter, now harbored the specter of uncertainty. A decision hung in the air, and Eddie, driven by a quest for truth, succumbed to the tug of curiosity.

The screen of Jennifer's phone unveiled a narrative that unfolded in calls and texts – a clandestine meeting with a mysterious Mike in the heart of the park. Eddie's heart, a captive audience, felt the weight of the revelation. The once vibrant colors of their day now bore the shades of doubt and betrayal.

Jennifer returned, her demeanor unchanged, yet Eddie (Vance) couldn't mask the turmoil within. He wrestled with the decision to confront her or retreat into the silent recesses of his thoughts. The oak tree, witness to their shared laughter, now stood sentinel to a moment of impending revelation.

As the day progressed, Eddie (Vance) and Jennifer navigated the park's pathways, their steps now accompanied by the unspoken tension between them. The laughter, once harmonious, now echoed with the dissonance of unspoken words. The sun, oblivious to the human drama unfolding below, continued its descent toward the horizon.

In the quiet corners of the park, Eddie (Vance) grappled with the unsettling truth, a truth that had the power to redefine their connection. The park, once a haven of shared moments, became a backdrop for the intricate dance of emotions – love, doubt, and the fragile threads that bound them together.

Little did Eddie (Vance) know that this day, filled with the hues of surprise and shared exploration, would mark the beginning of a journey into the complexities of human relationships. The sanctuary of the park would become a witness to their highs and lows.

Jennifer returned, her expression unchanged, and Eddie (Vance) couldn't bring himself to confront her immediately. They continued their day, laughter masking the tension beneath the surface.

As the afternoon sun bathed the park in warm hues, Eddie's (Vance’s) unease grew. He couldn't shake the feeling that something was amiss. Jennifer, however, seemed oblivious to his inner turmoil. They decided to take a break on a bench, and Eddie mustered the courage to address the elephant in the park.

"Jennifer, I couldn't help but notice the calls and texts from Mike earlier," Eddie (Vance) began cautiously.

Jennifer's eyes flickered with surprise, and a momentary hesitation crossed her face. "Oh, Mike? He's just a friend. We were planning to meet up later. Nothing serious."

Eddie (Vance), unsure whether to believe her, probed further. "Why didn't you mention it earlier?"

Jennifer sighed, her shoulders slumping. "I didn't think it was a big deal. We're just catching up. He's an old friend from my neighborhood."

As the sun began its descent, Eddie (Vance) couldn't shake the lingering unease. He wondered if he should have pressed the matter further or if he was overthinking the situation. The complexities of high school relationships and friendships added layers of uncertainty that neither of them anticipated.

As they parted ways that evening, Eddie (Vance) couldn't help but hope that Jennifer's explanation held true. The shadows of doubt, however, lingered in his mind, casting a subtle pall over what was supposed to be a carefree day.

In the days that followed, Eddie (Vance) couldn't shake off the feeling that something was amiss. Despite Jennifer's assurances, her frequent meetings with Mike became a cause for concern. Eddie (Vance) found himself grappling with a whirlwind of emotions – doubt, insecurity, and a growing sense of unease.

Unable to ignore the nagging suspicions, Eddie (Vance) decided to confront the issue head-on. One afternoon, he discreetly followed Jennifer to the park where she had arranged to meet Mike. As he discreetly approached the meeting spot, a knot tightened in his stomach, betraying the anxiety building within him.

Peering through the foliage, Eddie's (Vance's) worst fears materialized before his eyes. There, beneath the same oak tree where they had spent a carefree day together, Jennifer and Mike stood locked in an intimate embrace. The world around Eddie (Vance) seemed to fade into a blurry haze as he witnessed the very scene he had feared.

A surge of conflicting emotions overwhelmed him – disbelief, betrayal, and heartache. Eddie's (Vance's) hands trembled as he clutched the nearby branches for support. He had trusted Jennifer, given her the benefit of the doubt, and now, he felt the ground beneath him shatter.

Unable to tear his eyes away, Eddie (Vance) watched in stunned silence as Jennifer and Mike shared a kiss. The realization hit him like a tidal wave, leaving him gasping for air. The very park that once symbolized the innocence of their friendship became the backdrop to a heart-wrenching revelation.

As Jennifer and Mike parted ways, Eddie (Vance) wrestled with conflicting thoughts. Should he confront her immediately, or should he retreat and process the betrayal in solitude? The weight of the truth pressed upon him, making it difficult to breathe.

When Jennifer eventually noticed Eddie's (Vance's) presence, her eyes widened with guilt and surprise. Eddie's (Vance's) face, once adorned with a carefree smile, now bore the unmistakable marks of heartbreak. He couldn't find the words to express the depth of his emotions, and a heavy silence hung in the air between them.

Jennifer, unable to meet Eddie's (Vance’s) gaze, stammered out an apology. "Eddie, I... I didn't mean for you to find out like this."

The pain etched across Eddie’s (Vance's) face was undeniable. He finally mustered the strength to speak, his voice carrying a mix of anguish and disappointment. "I trusted you, Jennifer. I never expected this."

Without waiting for a response, Eddie (Vance) turned away, leaving Jennifer to grapple with the consequences of her actions. As he walked away from the scene of heartbreak, Eddie (Vance) couldn't help but mourn not only the loss of a friendship but also the innocence of his first relationship. The echoes of that fateful day lingered, casting a long shadow over what was once a vibrant connection between two souls.

***

In the aftermath of that heart-wrenching revelation in the park, Eddie (Vance) and Jennifer attempted to salvage the remains of their relationship. However, the wounds ran too deep, and the trust that had once bound them was irreparably shattered. As weeks turned into months, Eddie (Vance) grappled with a painful truth – the friendship they once cherished had crumbled, replaced by the debris of broken promises and unfulfilled trust.

One evening, as the sun dipped below the horizon, Eddie (Vance) and Jennifer sat down for a conversation that would alter the course of their lives. The weight of unspoken words hung in the air, and Eddie (Vance), with a heavy heart, acknowledged the inevitable.

"Jennifer, we need to talk," Eddie (Vance) began, his voice tinged with a mixture of sorrow and resignation.

Jennifer's eyes mirrored Vance's emotions, sensing the gravity of the moment. As Eddie (Vance) recounted the pain he had carried since that day in the park, the cracks in their relationship widened. It became evident that the wounds, though camouflaged by the passage of time, had never truly healed.

With a heavy sigh, Eddie (Vance) uttered the words that echoed the finality of their journey together. "I think it's time we let go. Our paths are diverging, and we need to find our own way."

With tears welling in her eyes, Jennifer nodded in reluctant agreement. The love they had once shared couldn't withstand the weight of unresolved pain, and they parted ways, acknowledging that some scars were meant to be carried alone.

In the aftermath of their breakup, Eddie (Vance) found himself engulfed in a sea of emotions. The pain of the past mingled with the grief of a lost future, creating a storm within his soul. He told himself that he would never move on, convinced that the scars from their shared history were too deep to be replaced.

Days turned into nights, and Eddie's (Vance's) resolve held firm. He immersed himself in the echoes of what once was, clinging to the remnants of a love that had withered away. The emotional turbulence within him mirrored the tempestuous weather outside, and Eddie found solace in the melancholy symphony of rain tapping against his window.

As he stared into the abyss of memories, Eddie (Vance) vowed to carry the weight of their shared past. The chapter with Jennifer had closed, but the emotional baggage lingered, a constant reminder of a love that had been both beautiful and tragic. In that moment of heartache, Eddie (Vance) told himself that moving on would be an act of betrayal to the depth of emotions he had invested in their relationship. Little did he know that time had a way of healing wounds, even the ones that seemed insurmountable.

Chapter 6

Caught in the unrelenting grasp of ceaseless anguish and internal turmoil, Eddie (Vance) found himself imprisoned by the shattered fragments of his emotions. His daily existence unfolded as a mechanical ballet, a predictable routine that involved attending college, going to work, and returning home to a solitude that had become an unyielding companion. Within this desolate realm, Eddie (Vance) cocooned himself in isolation, erecting barriers that shut out the world and repelled any attempts at meaningful conversation.

The haunting specter of Jennifer's betrayal cast a pervasive darkness over Eddie (Vance), akin to an ominous cloud that stubbornly lingered, refusing to dissipate. The mere contemplation of her infidelity gnawed at the core of his consciousness, draining him of the energy required to confront the painful reality or articulate the tumult of emotions to anyone who might lend a sympathetic ear.

Within this bleak landscape, the day unfolded, marked by a weariness that transcended the ordinary. Eddie (Vance) returned home, the physical manifestation of his exhaustion evident in every step, as if the burdens he bore had materialized into a tangible weight dragging him down. Seeking refuge from the relentless ache pulsating within, he reached for a few drinks, hoping to drown out the internal turmoil that threatened to engulf him.

The clinking of glasses and the soft murmur of liquid pouring provided a temporary respite, a momentary escape from the relentless grind of his emotional turmoil. In the amber hues of the liquid courage, Eddie (Vance) sought solace, attempting to numb the persistent ache that had become an unwelcome companion.

Yet, within the confines of this numbing ritual, Eddie(Vance)'s internal struggles persisted, their echoes resonating in the quiet corners of his mind. The haze of intoxication offered only a fleeting reprieve from the relentless grip of his emotions. The weight of betrayal, the monotony of routine, and the isolation he had woven around himself coalesced into an oppressive force, threatening to suffocate any semblance of peace.

As he wearily traversed the threshold into the living room, the scene that awaited him was a stark departure from the mundane. A gasp escaped his lips as his eyes widened in disbelief, and a single word hung in the air – "Hattie...?"

The silence that enveloped the room was held with the weight of something he had never experienced. Eddie (Vance), caught in the grip of astonishment, struggled to articulate the myriad thoughts racing through his mind.

As Eddie (Vance) took determined steps toward Hattie, a surge of concern enveloped him at the sight that unfolded before his eyes. He settled into a seat, his gaze fixated on her trembling form, the echo of her sobs filling the room. "Hattie, are you okay?" he gently inquired, his voice laced with genuine worry. However, Hattie remained silent, her tear-stained face a poignant testament to the pain she bore.

Driven by a mix of compassion and apprehension, Eddie (Vance) instinctively reached out to comfort her. His hands delicately cradled her shoulders, providing a subtle reassurance that she was not alone in this moment of vulnerability. Yet, as Eddie (Vance) sought solace in her presence, a disconcerting revelation emerged – a black eye marred Hattie's delicate features.

The shock of this discovery reverberated through Eddie (Vance), amplifying the concern etched across his face. "Hattie, who did this to you? Where's Earl?" Eddie (Vance)'s voice carried an undercurrent of anger, fueled by the protectiveness he felt towards someone who had once held a significant place in his life.

The prolonged silence from Hattie cast a somber shadow, accentuating the gravity of the situation. Her impassive stillness mirrored that of a mannequin, a silent observer amid the tumultuous emotions swirling around her. Through tearful eyes, she communicated a profound narrative of pain, a language that transcended the limitations of spoken words.

Eddie (Vance), undeterred by the walls of reticence, felt a surge of empathy propel him forward. With arms outstretched, he enveloped Hattie, forging a sanctuary within the storm that raged around them. Her tear-streaked face found solace against his chest, seeking refuge in the haven he offered amidst the chaos of their shared emotions.

In this intimate embrace, Eddie (Vance)'s fingers traced soothing patterns on Hattie's back, a wordless pledge to provide comfort in the absence of spoken language. The room, once a canvas for unresolved emotions, underwent a metamorphosis into a sanctuary where the language of touch surpassed the nuances of any conversation. Hattie, carrying the weight of unspoken agony, discovered a fleeting respite within Eddie(Vance)'s arms.

As time unfolded in suspended animation, Eddie (Vance) persisted in offering solace to Hattie. Each passing moment served as a poignant testament to the intricate dance of emotions that unfolded between them. Lingering questions hung in the air, their unresolved nature casting a cloak of uncertainty over the room. The mystery of Hattie's bruised state and the conspicuous absence of Earl permeated the atmosphere, leaving a tapestry of unanswered queries.

Despite the ambiguity, Eddie (Vance) remained steadfast in his commitment to console and support Hattie. The room became a crucible of emotions, a space where the unspoken could be felt more profoundly than any verbal exchange. The tender interplay of their connection echoed with a shared understanding, transcending the need for explicit answers.

As they navigated the uncharted terrain of emotions, Eddie (Vance) and Hattie found a delicate balance between vulnerability and strength. Once fraught with uncertainty, the room now resonated with the quiet assurance that they were not alone in confronting the complexities.

As the hands of the clock moved inexorably, Eddie (Vance) found himself cradling Hattie in a tender embrace that transcended mere moments. Patiently, he held her close, providing a silent sanctuary for the emotions that had long been concealed within the recesses of her heart. Time seemed to elongate, creating a space where Hattie could summon the strength to share a narrative that had remained shrouded in secrecy for far too long.

Amidst the quietude, their shared breaths resonated, creating a soft cadence that set the stage for Hattie's tentative yet resolute voice. Through tearful eyes, she unraveled a harrowing truth, exposing the sinister undercurrent that had marred her relationship with Earl. In the shadows of their shared existence, Earl's abusive tendencies had cast a looming darkness that Hattie had carried in stoic silence.

The gravity of her revelation weighed heavily on Eddie (Vance)'s heart, already burdened by his own internal struggles. As Hattie peeled back the layers of her anguish, Eddie(Vance)'s empathy deepened, bridging the chasm between their shared history and the present moment. The revelation pierced through the veil of his personal pain, igniting a profound sense of responsibility to shield the woman he had once held close.

In this moment of shared vulnerability, Eddie (Vance) became not only a witness to Hattie's suffering but also a guardian determined to offer solace and protection. The intricate dance of their emotions unfolded against the backdrop of a story that transcended individual tribulations. Eddie (Vance), compelled by compassion, felt a renewed commitment to stand between Hattie and the horrors that had scarred her past.

The weight of responsibility settled on Eddie(Vance)'s shoulders as he grappled with the profound implications of Hattie's revelations. Yet, within that weight, there existed an unwavering resolve to be a source of strength and support.

As the minutes turned into hours, Eddie (Vance)'s embrace became a haven for Hattie, a place where the burdens of the past could be momentarily set aside. Their shared breaths forged a connection that transcended spoken language, allowing the unspoken nuances of understanding to permeate the room. In the crucible of vulnerability, Eddie (Vance) and Hattie began a journey of healing, each step an affirmation of their shared commitment to move forward from the shadows of their painful past.

"I won't ever let Earl get close to you again. Don't worry," Eddie (Vance) reassured her, his voice carrying a solemn promise. The declaration was underscored by a fierce determination to shield Hattie from the looming shadows of her past. "You're safe now," he affirmed, each word resonating with an unyielding commitment to be her sanctuary in a world that had been unkind.

Wrapped in the cocoon of Eddie (Vance)'s unwavering support, Hattie nodded in silent acknowledgment, an unspoken agreement forged within the crucible of their shared pain. Their embrace became a sanctuary, a haven of profound security amid the turbulent storms that had relentlessly battered their lives.

With a gentle touch, Eddie (Vance) guided Hattie to bed, a sacred space where she could seek refuge from the physical and emotional bruises that marked her existence. As she settled into the comforting embrace of the mattress, Eddie (Vance)'s tender ministrations tended to her black eye, each gesture a reflection of the healing balm of empathy. The room, once a witness to anguish, underwent a metamorphosis into a cocoon of compassion, where the shared vulnerability of two souls found solace in each other's company.

As Hattie succumbed to the peaceful embrace of sleep, Eddie (Vance) assumed the role of a silent guardian, standing watch over her serenity. In the hushed stillness of the night, a glimmer of hope unfurled – the promise of a new chapter, where the haunting echoes of pain would gradually give way to the gentle notes of healing and renewal.

The room, imbued with a newfound tranquility, became a silent witness to the beginning of a journey towards healing. Eddie (Vance)'s vigilant presence symbolized not just protection but also a commitment to stand by Hattie as she navigated the labyrinth of her own recovery. In the quietude, a subtle transformation occurred, marking the inception of a narrative where the resilience of the human spirit triumphed over the shadows of adversity.

As the night unfolded, Eddie (Vance)'s watchful gaze bore witness to the delicate interplay of dreams and memories that danced across Hattie's slumbering mind. The promise of a brighter tomorrow lay dormant in the whispers of the night, waiting to be unraveled as the dawn heralded the advent of a new day.

In this moment of repose, Eddie (Vance) and Hattie embarked on a shared journey of renewal, where the tenderness of empathy and the silent language of touch served as guiding stars. The cocoon of compassion they had woven around themselves became a sanctuary where healing was not just an aspiration but a tangible reality, gradually transforming the echoes of pain into a melodic symphony of hope and resilience.

Chapter 7

The subsequent day marked an unexpected deviation from Eddie (Vance)'s usual routine. Typically a determined pillar of strength, he was now succumbing to the grips of the flu, necessitating a departure from his customary activities. The cadence of his life, which usually involved attending college, fulfilling work commitments, and savoring solitary moments, was abruptly disrupted by the unwelcome intrusion of illness.

Hattie, despite the intricacies embedded in their shared history, stepped forward to tend to Eddie (Vance). She assumed the role of caregiver, eclipsing her customary position as the one in need of care. Going above and beyond the call of duty, Hattie took it upon herself to prepare nourishing soup, its' comforting aroma permeating the air and imbuing the atmosphere with a sense of solace.

"This is my secret recipe, y'know. It'll help you recover in no time," she told Eddie (Vance), handing him the bowl. Poor Eddie (Vance) could hardly manage a 'thank you' in between sneezes. This unanticipated act of care represented a departure from the norm, a poignant reversal of roles as Hattie embraced the responsibility of tending to Eddie (Vance) in his moment of vulnerability.

Throughout the quiet interludes of sickness, Hattie's actions resonated deeply, transcending the realm of mere gestures. They unfurled as a testament to the profound connection between Eddie (Vance) and Hattie.

As the flu enforced a pause in Eddie (Vance)'s relentless pursuits, the space created as a result allowed for a delicate recalibration of their relationship. The dawn that followed Eddie (Vance)'s night of sickness not only heralded the promise of physical recovery but also symbolized the emergence of a renewed and strengthened bond anchored in mutual care and reciprocity.

This unexpected pause due to the flu became an opportunity for Eddie (Vance) and Hattie to forge a more profound connection. In their moments of vulnerability, they discovered common ground, silently understanding each other without the need for extensive conversation. The soup that Hattie prepared went beyond its physical healing properties; it symbolized a fresh start for both of them.

As the day unfolded, marked by moments of recovery and shared care, Eddie (Vance) and Hattie stood at the threshold of a new beginning. The promise of a brighter tomorrow, hinted at during the preceding quiet night, began to materialize in the simple acts of kindness and understanding exchanged within their shared space. Unbeknownst to them, the unexpected convergence during a period of vulnerability pointed toward the possibility of a future where the echoes of past pain could be supplanted by the gradual, melodic notes of healing and renewal.

On a day when Earl was away for work, Eddie (Vance) and Hattie found themselves alone at home; however, the unexpected development that was to follow would reshape their relationship.

In the morning, Eddie (Vance), unaware of Hattie's presence, felt the need to go to the bathroom. Unintentionally breaching her privacy, he walked in on Hattie emerging from the shower.

"Oh, I'm sorry," Eddie (Vance) apologized as he entered the room, catching Hattie in the midst of her post-shower routine. Hattie responded with a nonchalant shrug, indicating that his presence wasn't an unwelcome intrusion. Instead of making a hasty exit, Eddie (Vance) decided to use the bathroom while Hattie continued with her routine.

The unexpected closeness between them served as a catalyst for an unforeseen, intimate moment. A subtle shift in the air drew them together, and before either of them fully comprehended the change in dynamics, their lips met in a kiss. It was a merging of unspoken desires and emotions that had lingered beneath the surface, and in that moment, the outside world seemed to dissolve as they surrendered to the tide of emotions.

Vulnerability and passion intertwined, creating an emotional tapestry neither Eddie nor Hattie had anticipated. The room, dimly lit and filled with the aftermath of their connection, encapsulated the depth of the experience.

Entwined in each other's arms, they lay there, the night enveloping their newfound connection. The unexpected development added a layer of complexity to their relationship, injecting an intricate element into the fabric of their connection. This unforeseen intimacy became a secret shared between them, an unexpected twist that would forever alter the trajectory of their lives. As they embraced the complexity of their newfound connection, Eddie and Hattie were left to navigate the uncharted territories of their evolving relationship.

This seemingly commonplace incident carried a subtle yet profound significance. It acted as a catalyst for change, pushing the boundaries of their familiarity and establishing a newfound level of comfort between them. Though initially marked by awkwardness, the incident became a moment of unspoken understanding, setting the stage for a future where vulnerability and acceptance would shape the trajectory of their evolving connection. In this unplanned intersection of their lives, Eddie (Vance) and Hattie unwittingly embarked on a journey with the potential to transform their relationship into a canvas where healing and renewal could gradually paint over the layers of past pain.

As the day unfolded, Eddie (Vance) and Hattie grappled with the implications of their newfound intimacy. The air hung heavy with mixed emotions, and their conversations carried unspoken feelings about the uncharted territory they had entered. The encounter prompted them to confront the complexities that had surfaced, challenging them to navigate this unanticipated turn in their relationship.

In the subsequent moments, Eddie (Vance) and Hattie found themselves at a crossroads, unsure of what lay ahead for them. The unplanned intimacy had laid bare the vulnerabilities and intricacies woven into the fabric of their connection. Their conversations, now laden with unspoken emotions, became a bridge between the known and the unknown as they endeavored to make sense of the uncharted territory they had stepped into.

The day that began with an unintentional intrusion unfolded into a transformative chapter in Eddie (Vance) and Hattie's relationship. The complexity of their emotions and the unexplored terrain they now traversed set the stage for a journey that would require courage, introspection, and a willingness to embrace the uncertainty that lay ahead.

In the following days, Eddie (Vance) and Hattie found themselves walking a delicate tightrope between the familiar and the unknown. The weight of contemplation pressed upon them as they grappled with the question of where to go from that intimate juncture. The past they shared and the present circumstances served as the backdrop for their silent negotiation – hearts yearning for connection, yet minds cautious about the potential consequences of traversing uncharted emotional territories.

Amidst the intricacies of this emotional journey, Eddie (Vance) and Hattie discovered a unique space where honesty and vulnerability could coexist. The accidental intimacy became a pivotal starting point for open conversations about their feelings, fears, and the intricate web of their shared history. Navigating this uncharted path, Eddie (Vance) and Hattie, in their shared vulnerability, started to unravel the complexities of their relationship. They explored the layers that had long remained concealed, confronting uncomfortable truths and acknowledging the intricacies that had shaped the contours of their connection.

As the days unfolded, their conversations became a lifeline, allowing them to dissect the nuances of their emotions and intentions. The unexpected intimacy, while initially a source of complexity, served as a catalyst for a deeper understanding between them. They began to discern the intricate dance of desires and reservations within their hearts, creating a roadmap for navigating the uncharted waters of their relationship.

Hattie found herself intricately linked not only to Vance (Eddie), who happened to be Eddie (Vance)'s best friend, but also to Jennifer, Eddie (Vance)'s ex-girlfriend. This familial connection added an extra layer of complexity to an already intricate situation. Eddie (Vance) stood at the crossroads of these complexities, grappling with the dilemma of whether to forge ahead or take a step back.

The intertwining familial ties with their newfound intimacy created a web of considerations that added a nuanced dimension to Eddie (Vance)'s contemplation. The delicate balance between personal desires and the potential impact on existing relationships became a pivotal factor in his decision-making process. Uncertain of the implications, he found himself at the nexus of these complexities, torn between venturing into uncharted emotional territory and the potential repercussions on his longstanding friendship with Vance (Eddie).

The relational dynamics and loyalties at play intensified Eddie (Vance)'s internal struggle. The evolving narrative of Eddie (Vance) and Hattie's relationship now faced the added challenge of navigating familial connections, introducing a layer of intricacy that demanded careful consideration and reflection. The prospect of affecting not just a friendship but also familial ties weighed heavily on Eddie (Vance)'s mind as he navigated the complex landscape of emotions and relationships.

The evolving relationship between Eddie (Vance) and Hattie became a delicate balance, with each step forward requiring thoughtful consideration of the connections that wove their lives together. The complexities of their intertwined relationships demanded a heightened awareness of the potential impact, making every decision a nuanced exploration of emotions and loyalties.

The future they faced remained shrouded in uncertainty, but Eddie (Vance) and Hattie found solace in the honesty and openness they cultivated. The journey they embarked upon, spurred by an accidental moment of intimacy, became a shared exploration of their emotional landscape. In their joint vulnerability, they took steps toward a future where the only certainty was the unpredictability ahead.

Chapter 8

As Earl's work trips became more frequent, his travels provided a fertile ground for the blossoming affair between Eddie (Vance) and Hattie. The allure of stolen moments and secret encounters became intoxicating, heightening the intensity of their connection with each rendezvous.

In the hushed hours when Earl's presence was replaced by a silence that amplified the sounds of their whispers and shared laughter, Eddie (Vance) and Hattie found themselves navigating the delicate tightrope between the forbidden and the irresistible. The quietness of those moments, punctuated only by the distant hum of the outside world, became the backdrop to their passionate escapades.

The stolen moments unfolded like chapters in a novel, each meeting marked by a shared anticipation and a sense of urgency. Their passion, hidden behind closed doors and veiled glances, flourished in the secrecy of Earl's absence. The very act of keeping their connection concealed added an element of thrill, a sense of rebellion that fueled the flames of desire between them.

The forbidden nature of their affair cast a magnetic spell, drawing them closer in the face of societal norms and moral constraints. The stolen kisses, lingering touches, and shared glances became a language of their own.

In the haven they had created, Eddie (Vance) and Hattie sought refuge from the complexities of their external lives. The stolen moments provided not only an escape from reality but also a sanctuary where their desires could unfold freely. The secret affair thrived in the quiet hours in Earl's absence, allowing the connection between Eddie (Vance) and Hattie to bloom.

However, one fateful day, the routine was disrupted. Earl returned home unexpectedly, cutting short his work trip. The door creaked open, and there stood Earl, a mix of shock and betrayal etched across his face. Time seemed to freeze as Eddie (Vance) and Hattie, caught in the act, faced the consequences of their secret liaison.

"Earl, I... I can explain," Eddie (Vance) stammered, guilt and panic evident in his eyes as he attempted to rise from the awkward position he found himself in with Hattie.

Hattie, her face flushed with embarrassment and remorse, attempted to find words to placate the brewing storm. "Earl, it's not what it looks like. We didn't mean for you to find out this way," she pleaded, her voice strained with emotion.

Earl's gaze shifted between Eddie (Vance) and Hattie, a mix of disbelief and hurt clouding his features. "Not what it looks like?" he asked, his tone a blend of anger and disappointment. "How long has this been going on? How could you, Eddie? And you, Hattie?!"

Realizing the gravity of the situation, Eddie (Vance) struggled to find the right words. "Earl, it's complicated. We never meant to hurt you," he muttered, his attempt at an explanation falling short in the face of Earl's justified outrage.

With tears welling up in her eyes, Hattie reached out to Earl. "We didn't plan for any of this. It just... happened," she confessed, her voice shaky with remorse.

The room became charged with tension as Earl's voice thundered through the silence, demanding an explanation. Hattie, now confronted with the harsh reality of her actions, struggled to find words to justify the affair.

"Explain yourselves! How could you betray me like this?" Earl's voice boomed, echoing through the room.

Hattie's eyes were downcast, and her hands were nervously fidgeting. "Earl, it's not as simple as it seems. We never intended for things to turn out like this."

The air crackled with the weight of unspoken truths and the consequences of their choices. Earl's gaze bore into both Eddie (Vance) and Hattie, a mix of anger and disbelief etched across his face.

The discussion turned into a heated confrontation, with Earl expressing a mixture of hurt, anger, and disbelief. Hattie, torn between remorse and the desire for the forbidden, found herself in the center of a storm. Before anyone could react, Earl slapped Hattie across the room. Frozen and unable to confront him, Eddie (Vance) just stared at the chaos unfolding.

The resounding slap echoed through the room, leaving a tense silence in its wake. Hattie, staggered by the force of the blow, clutched her cheek, eyes brimming with a mixture of pain and shock. Earl's face twisted with a volatile mix of anger and frustration. His actions were fueled by a sense of betrayal that had ignited a tempest within him.

"HOW COULD YOU DO THIS TO ME?!" Earl shouted, his voice laced with a bitter intensity. "I trusted you, Hattie, and this is how you repay me?"

Hattie’s face was flushed, and her eyes glistened with unshed tears. She managed to find her voice as she pleaded, "Earl, please, let me explain."

But Earl, consumed by a righteous fury, seemed deaf to her pleas. Another wave of anger surged through him, and before anyone could react, his hand struck out again. This time, the force of the slap sent Hattie stumbling backward, colliding with a piece of furniture.

Eddie (Vance) felt a sickening knot tighten in his stomach. He wanted to intervene, to protect Hattie from further harm, but the weight of guilt and the complexity of their entangled relationships had paralyzed him.

As the fight raged on, Eddie (Vance) grappled with conflicting emotions – a sense of responsibility for the turmoil he had unintentionally triggered and the helplessness of not being able to stop the escalating violence. The once-intimate connections between them now unraveled in a tumultuous storm of emotions, leaving scars that would linger long after the physical altercation subsided.

"I trusted you, Hattie! And you, Eddie (Vance), how could you do this?" Earl's frustration escalated, his emotions reaching a boiling point.

Eddie (Vance), his guilt palpable, tried to interject, "Earl, I never meant for any of this to happen. It's a mess, and I'm sorry."

Accusations flew like daggers, each word cutting deeper into the already strained relationships. Earl's sense of betrayal clashed with Hattie's internal conflict and Eddie (Vance)'s realization of the impact on both his friendship with Vance (Eddie) and familial ties.

"Earl, we messed up, but it's not too late to fix things. We can work through this together," Hattie was still pleading. Her voice was strained with both desperation and hope, and her eyes desperately searched for a glimmer of understanding in Earl's anguished expression.

However, Earl, still seething with a mix of betrayal and fury, seemed unyielding. "Fix things? How do you propose we fix this, Hattie?" he retorted, his tone bitter and resentful. The echoes of their heated confrontation lingered in the air, each word a painful reminder of the shattered trust that once bound them together.

The emotional turbulence of that moment continued to reverberate in the shattered remnants of trust. The room, once a sanctuary for secrets, now bore witness to the wreckage of their relationships. The consequences of their choices cast a long, dark shadow over the tangled web they had woven, leaving scars that extended beyond the physical altercation.

Eddie (Vance), caught in the crossfire of guilt and regret, finally found his voice. "We need to figure out how to move forward from here. This can't be the end of everything."

Earl turned his gaze toward Vance, his expression a mixture of sadness and disappointment. "You should have thought about that before you slept with my wife, you bastard!" With that, in a sudden, violent motion, Earl swung his fist at Eddie, connecting with his jaw in a forceful punch.

Vance, taken aback by the unexpected assault, stumbled backward, his hand instinctively covering the stinging mark on his jaw. The room was now charged with an even more palpable tension as the violence escalated. Earl's frustration manifested in a physical outburst against both Eddie (Vance) and Hattie.

Gripping onto Eddie (Vance)'s collar, Earl dragged him out to the stairway, spouting whatever curse words he could at that moment. Eddie (Vance) felt he should have done something to protect Hattie.

"LET GO!" Eddie (Vance) screamed at the top of his lungs, trying to break free from his restraints. Earl raised his fist yet again to attack to strike Eddie (Vance) but he was stopped midway, as Eddie (Vance) overpowered Earl and pushed him down the stairway. A series of horrifying thuds echoed through the house, followed by silence, marking the tragic end to their tumultuous confrontation. Earl's lifeless body lay at the foot of the stairs, blood pooling around him.

Eddie (Vance), with panic and shock etched across his face, rushed to Earl's side. He was desperate to find any sign of life. "Earl! Earl, wake up!" he exclaimed, his voice trembling with a mixture of fear and regret.

Hattie was equally stricken with the weight of guilt and the consequences of their actions and stood frozen in disbelief. "Oh no, Eddie! No, no, no! What have we done?" she muttered, her eyes wide with horror as she witnessed the unfolding tragedy.

The once-intimate affair that had been a secret source of joy and passion had now morphed into an unforeseen tragedy that neither Eddie (Vance) nor Hattie could have predicted. The room echoed with the urgency of Eddie (Vance)'s pleas, while Hattie stood silent in shock as she grappled with the magnitude of their choices.

As Eddie (Vance) desperately checked for a pulse and tried to revive Earl, Hattie whispered in a trembling voice, "We need to call for help. Now!"

The weight of the situation pressed upon them. Eddie (Vance), still in shock, nodded in agreement and looked around for his phone, then dialed 911.

The wailing sirens of the approaching ambulance shattered the uneasy silence that hung in the aftermath of Earl's fall. The paramedics rushed into the house, their urgency reflecting the severity of the situation. Hattie and Eddie (Vance) stepped aside as the EMTs worked to assess Earl's condition.

The paramedics quickly determined the extent of Earl's injuries and informed he was to be moved to a hospital right away. It was a heartbreaking realization – the injuries sustained from the fall were too severe, and their efforts to revive him proved futile. Earl, an 80-year-old man whose life had taken an unexpected turn, succumbed to the consequences of that ill-fated push down the stairs.

As the ambulance sped toward the hospital, the realization of the irreparable loss began to sink in.

As the police arrived at the hospital with the ambulance, Eddie (Vance) and Hattie exchanged anxious glances. The officers, stern-faced and inquisitive, took them to a private room to begin their investigation, questioning them about the events leading up to Earl's fall.

Detective Simmons, taking charge of the situation, turned to Eddie (Vance) and Hattie. "Can you walk us through what happened here?"

Eddie (Vance), his voice shaky and eyes avoiding direct contact, responded, "We had just come back from running errands when we found Earl like this. When we saw him lying there and bleeding out, we called 911 right away."

Mirroring Eddie (Vance)'s distress, Hattie added, "Yes, we didn't hear anything, and when we got home, the door was slightly ajar. We rushed in, fearing someone had broken in, but we found Earl lying on the floor, bleeding."

Detective Simmons furrowed his brow, scrutinizing their every word. "Did either of you notice anything unusual before you left or when you returned?"

Eddie (Vance) hesitated before replying, "No, everything seemed normal. Earl was fine when we left."

Detective Simmons continued, "And how would you explain the state of the stairs? Any signs of a struggle?"

"No, officer. We didn't see anything out of the ordinary. Maybe he just lost his footing?" Hattie suggested in a quivering voice.

Both of them started to weave their fabricated story into the investigation, the foundation upon which they hoped to build a defense against the looming consequences.

Detective Simmons appeared to be satisfied with their explanation, and he nodded. "Well, we'll need you both to come down to the station to provide official statements."

Eddie (Vance) and Hattie exchanged relieved glances; the weight of their lies temporarily lifted. As the investigation unfolded, Eddie (Vance) and Hattie continued to play their parts convincingly, offering a seamless narrative that concealed the tumultuous events preceding Earl's fall.

As the police investigation continued and the news of Earl's death spread, the weight of guilt and remorse pressed upon Eddie (Vance) and Hattie. The consequences of their actions had far-reaching implications, extending beyond the legal repercussions to the emotional toll on those left behind. Earl's sudden and tragic end marked not only the conclusion of life but also the beginning of a harrowing journey for those entangled in the web of secrets and lies.

Chapter 9

As weeks turned into months, Eddie (Vance) found solace in the routine of his job, burying himself in the day-to-day tasks to escape the haunting memories of Earl’s death. However, the weight of guilt and the burden of his actions took a toll on his mental well-being. The facade of normalcy he maintained in public was a stark contrast to the internal struggle he faced daily.

His nights were filled with restless sleep, plagued by nightmares that replayed the tragic events leading up to Earl's death. Echoes of his conscience whispered accusations, forcing Eddie (Vance) to question the choices that had led to that fateful moment. Drinking and smoking only provided temporary relief, serving as a fleeting escape from the reality he tried desperately to evade.

On the other hand, it seemed Hattie’s life was finally getting better. The insurance money she had received was enough to cover her expenses, and she had somehow managed to maintain a semblance of a normal life, seemingly untouched by the consequences of their actions. Her composed demeanor hid the guilt that Eddie (Vance) struggled to conceal.

As the investigation wore on, Detective Simmons grew increasingly suspicious. Despite the seemingly airtight statements from Eddie (Vance) and Hattie, there were subtle inconsistencies that raised flags in his mind. The detective decided to dig deeper, determined to uncover the truth that lingered beneath the surface.

Meanwhile, Eddie (Vance)'s internal struggle escalated, leading him to seek professional help. He started attending therapy sessions, attempting to navigate the complex emotions that had taken root within him. The therapist became his confidant, and through the process, Eddie (Vance) gradually began to confront the reality of his actions.

Hattie, unaware of Eddie (Vance)'s turmoil, continued to navigate the aftermath with a calculated poise. She maintained the appearance of a grieving widow, attending public events and gatherings with a facade of composure. However, the shadows of guilt began to creep into her thoughts, and she found herself feeling increasingly isolated, the weight of her secrets becoming harder to bear.

In the midst of their shared struggles, a peculiar bond formed between Hattie and Eddie (Vance). Despite the weight of guilt and the looming threat of Detective Simmons uncovering the truth, Hattie continued to care for Eddie (Vance) in a way that transcended the boundaries of their initial agreement.

One evening, as the sun dipped below the horizon, casting long shadows over their shared secrets, Hattie found Eddie (Vance) sitting alone, staring blankly into the distance. The air was heavy with unspoken words, and Hattie hesitated before breaking the silence.

"Eddie, I know it's been tough for both of us. We never expected things to turn out this way," Hattie spoke as she looked at him from a distance.

Eddie (Vance)looked up, his eyes reflecting a mixture of pain and gratitude. The acknowledgment of their shared burden created a unique understanding between them.

"Yeah, it's been hell. I never thought I'd find myself in such a mess," sighing, Eddie (Vance) responded.

Hattie took a seat beside him, the weight of their experiences creating a silent connection. "We need each other, Eddie. We can't keep pretending that everything's fine. Let's face this together."

As they navigated the complexities of their emotions, Hattie opened up about her own struggles. The facade of composure she presented to the world began to crack, revealing a vulnerability that mirrored Vance's inner turmoil.

"I thought I could handle it all, but the guilt... it eats at me. I never wanted any of this," Hattie responded as she began tearing up.

Touched by her honesty, Eddie (Vance) extended a comforting hand. "We're in this together, Hattie. No more hiding, no more lies. It's time we confront our actions and open up to each other. I want us to be honest with each other."

The shared burden brought them closer, and as they faced the darkness within themselves, an unexpected intimacy blossomed. Their connection went beyond the surface, evolving into a genuine understanding that surpassed the confines of their initial arrangement.

Hattie's unwavering care for Eddie (Vance) became a beacon of support amid the shadows of guilt and deception. Despite the weight of their shared secrets, Hattie demonstrated a surprising depth of compassion. In an unexpected turn, she decided to share the insurance benefits with Eddie (Vance).

The financial support extended beyond mere provision, as Eddie (Vance), burdened by guilt and the emotional aftermath of Earl's death, found solace in Hattie's gesture. The money helped cover his school expenses and facilitated his therapy sessions, a crucial lifeline in navigating the storm of emotions that threatened to engulf him.

In turn, Eddie (Vance) assumed the role of Hattie's caretaker, providing companionship and assistance that went beyond the surface of their arrangement. The exchange of roles and responsibilities became a silent pact, a mutual understanding that strengthened their connection in the face of adversity. Their lives intertwined, and each of them relied on the other to navigate the complexities of guilt and remorse.

One evening, after a particularly revealing therapy session for Eddie (Vance), he found himself standing in his living room, the weight of his grief palpable. In a moment of vulnerability, Hattie reached out, pulling Eddie (Vance) into a heartfelt hug. The embrace lingered, providing a sense of solace and mutual support that neither had experienced since the tragic events unfolded.

Eddie (Vance), overwhelmed by the mix of emotions, looked into Hattie's eyes, and in that shared gaze, they found a moment of solace and understanding. It was a turning point, a cathartic release from the shackles of guilt that had bound them for so long.

"Thank you, Hattie," he spoke softly.

"We're in this together, Eddie. We'll find a way to navigate through it, no matter how difficult it gets," she reassured him, rubbing his back.

As they continued to lean on each other for support, the grief that once consumed them began to dissipate. Their connection evolved into a source of strength, helping them confront the truth and face the consequences of their actions with a newfound resilience. The journey ahead was uncertain, but together, they found a glimmer of hope in the midst of their shared despair.

Their dynamic evolved beyond the exchange of financial support as Eddie (Vance) took on additional responsibilities to ease Hattie's burden. They found themselves engaged in discussions about practical matters, planning how Eddie (Vance) would assist her with tasks around the house and serve as her chauffeur when needed.

Hattie was grateful for Eddie (Vance)'s willingness to lend a helping hand and discussed the logistics of their arrangement with him. They strategized on how Eddie (Vance)could efficiently manage his academic pursuits while fulfilling his role as her caretaker. The conversations were pragmatic yet tinged with a sense of mutual understanding and appreciation for each other's contributions.

As they delved deeper into their shared responsibilities, Eddie (Vance) embraced his role with a newfound sense of purpose. He found fulfillment in providing practical assistance, whether it was driving Hattie to appointments or tackling handyman tasks around the house. These acts of service became a tangible expression of their evolving relationship, strengthening the bond that had formed amidst the chaos of their shared secrets.

For Hattie, Eddie (Vance)'s support went beyond mere assistance with chores. It was a testament to their growing connection, a reminder that amidst the guilt and remorse, there was still room for compassion and understanding. Their discussions about practical matters became a source of comfort, a reminder that they were not alone in navigating the challenges that lay ahead.

They moved forward, hand in hand, navigating the twists and turns of life, finding solace in each other's presence. In the midst of their shared grief and guilt, they found a glimmer of hope in the simple act of supporting each other through the trials that lay ahead.

Seizing a rare opportunity for respite, Eddie (Vance) and Hattie hatched a plan to escape the suffocating atmosphere of their shared secrets. While Vance (Eddie) was spending time with his girlfriend, Eddie (Vance) and Hattie embarked on a three-day journey to Atlantic City, a place where the weight of their burdens could momentarily be set aside.

The decision to keep their escapade a secret from those around them added an element of spontaneity and thrill to their getaway. Eddie (Vance), usually burdened by guilt and remorse, found a temporary reprieve in the idea of leaving their troubles behind, even if it was just for a short while. Hattie, too, relished the prospect of a break from the facade she maintained in public.

As they cruised down the highway in Eddie (Vance)'s car, the wind carrying away the whispers of their shared past, a sense of liberation washed over them. The neon lights of Atlantic City greeted them like beacons of temporary freedom, a stark contrast to the shadows that lingered back home. The buzz of the casino floors and the salty breeze from the ocean served as a backdrop for a few days of reprieve.

In the heart of Atlantic City, Eddie (Vance) and Hattie found peace in secrecy. They strolled along the boardwalk, shared laughter over meals, and even tried their luck at the slot machines. The weight of guilt seemed to lift, if only for a moment, as they immersed themselves in the distractions the city offered.

Their secret trip became a sanctuary, a shared secret that bound them closer together. The unspoken understanding of the temporary escape brought an unexpected intimacy, allowing them to momentarily forget the tangled web of lies and deceit they left behind.

Yet, as the days in Atlantic City dwindled, a looming reality awaited their return. The journey back home would bring with it the resumption of their roles and responsibilities and the weight of guilt resuming its place on their shoulders.

Chapter 10

Eddie (Vance) felt a tug of nostalgia as he drove down the familiar streets of his hometown. After being away for four years for college, he was back again, this time with a mission. It was his final year, and the impending reality of graduation weighed heavily on his mind. With student loans piling up and uncertain job prospects in the city where his college was located, he made the decision to return to where it all began.

The small town hadn't changed much, yet Eddie (Vance) found himself seeing it through new eyes. There was a quaint charm to the place, a comforting familiarity that he had missed while being away. As he passed by the local diner where he used to hang out with friends, memories flooded back, reminding him of simpler times.

But nostalgia couldn't overshadow his purpose. Eddie (Vance) was here for a reason—to find a job. He knew it wouldn't be easy in a town where opportunities were limited compared to the bustling city he had grown accustomed to. Yet, there was a sense of determination burning within him. He refused to let his college years end with uncertainty and debt.

With resumes in hand, Eddie (Vance) embarked on his job hunt. He knocked on doors, filled out applications, and attended interviews, all the while hoping for a chance to prove himself. Despite the challenges, he remained optimistic, drawing strength from the support of his family and the community he had known all his life.

Weeks turned into months, and just when doubt started to creep in, Eddie (Vance) received the news he had been waiting for—a job offer from a local company. It wasn't the glamorous career he had once envisioned, but it was a start, a foothold in the professional world.

As he accepted the offer, Eddie (Vance) realized that returning to his hometown wasn't just about finding a job; it was about rediscovering his roots, reconnecting with his past, and embracing the future with open arms. As he settled into his new role, he knew that no matter where life took him next, this town would always hold a special place in his heart.

Despite the changes and challenges, one thing remained constant in Eddie (Vance)'s life—his friendship with Vance (Eddie). From childhood adventures to college escapades, they had been through it all together. So, they made sure to stay in touch.

Their reunions were filled with laughter and reminiscing about old times. They spent their days off exploring familiar haunts, revisiting their favorite spots, and discovering new ones. Whether it was hiking in the nearby woods, grabbing burgers at the diner, or simply lounging around playing video games, Eddie (Vance) and Vance (Eddie) cherished every moment spent together.

Their friendship was a source of comfort and joy amidst the uncertainties of post-grad life. They supported each other through the highs and lows, offering encouragement and lending a listening ear whenever needed. Eddie (Vance) found solace in

Vance (Eddie)'s unwavering presence, knowing that no matter what the future held, their bond would endure.

In each other's company, Eddie (Vance) and Vance (Eddie) found a sense of belonging and purpose, reaffirming the importance of friendship in shaping their lives. And as they embarked on new adventures together, they knew that their bond would continue to grow stronger with each passing day.

There was a secret weighing on Eddie (Vance)'s mind, one he hadn't yet found the courage to share with his best friend, Vance (Eddie). Eddie (Vance) and Hattie were still going strong, keeping their relationship hidden from the world.

Their love blossomed in stolen glances and whispered conversations, hidden away from prying eyes. Eddie (Vance) found himself drawn to Hattie's laughter, her kindness, and the way her eyes sparkled in the sunlight. And Hattie, in turn, was captivated by Eddie (Vance)'s charm, his unwavering support, and the way he made her feel like the most important person in the world.

Despite their deepening connection, Eddie (Vance) and Hattie made a mutual decision to keep their romance under wraps, at least for now. They feared that revealing their relationship might change the dynamics of Eddie (Vance)'s friendship with Vance (Eddie). They cherished their time together in secret, relishing the thrill of forbidden love while they navigated the complexities of their budding romance.

Yet, as they stole moments together in the quiet corners of his hometown, Eddie (Vance) couldn't shake the guilt of keeping such a significant part of his life hidden from Vance (Eddie), his closest friend. He knew that eventually, the truth would have to come out, but for now, he was content to bask in the warmth of their secret love, hoping that one day soon, he would find the courage to share it with his best friend and the world.

On a serene evening, as Eddie (Vance) and Hattie strolled through the familiar streets, Eddie (Vance)'s heart swelled with affection for the woman by his side. As they walked hand in hand, the gentle breeze carrying whispers of their shared laughter, Eddie (Vance) felt a surge of courage welling within him.

With a tender smile, he stopped in front of a quaint jewelry store, its windows adorned with glimmering treasures. Hattie glanced at him curiously, her eyes shining with curiosity as Eddie (Vance) led her inside. Amidst the soft glow of the store, Eddie (Vance)'s gaze fell upon a delicate ring, simple yet elegant—a perfect symbol of their love.

With a nervous breath, Eddie (Vance) took Hattie's hand in his and placed the ring on her finger, his voice trembling slightly as he spoke words of affection. It was a friendship ring, he explained, a token of their bond and the depth of his feelings for her.

Hattie's eyes widened in surprise, her heart overflowing with warmth at Eddie (Vance)'s heartfelt gesture. She embraced him tightly, her eyes brimming with tears of joy as she whispered words of love and gratitude.

At that moment, amidst the soft glow of the store and the warmth of their embrace, Eddie (Vance) and Hattie forged a deeper connection, their love solidified by the simple yet profound act of exchanging friendship rings. As they continued their stroll through the streets, hand in hand, they knew that their love was a treasure worth cherishing, a bond that would endure the test of time.

***

The tranquility of Vance (Eddie)'s family life was shattered by a storm of betrayal and heartbreak when Susan, Vance (Eddie)'s mother, uncovered the painful truth about her husband's infidelity. It was a devastating blow that tore apart the very fabric of their once-happy home.

Caught in the throes of anguish and disbelief, Susan made the gut-wrenching decision to confront her husband, her voice trembling with a mixture of anger and hurt as she demanded answers. And as the painful truth came to light, Vance (Eddie)'s world crumbled around him.

The once unshakeable foundation of his family was shattered, replaced by a sense of turmoil and uncertainty that threatened to engulf them all. Vance (Eddie) struggled to come to terms with the betrayal, grappling with emotions of anger, confusion, and sorrow as he watched his parents' marriage unravel before his eyes.

As the dust settled and the reality of their fractured family sank in, Vance (Eddie) found himself navigating uncharted territory, caught between the conflicting emotions of loyalty to his mother and the pain of his father's betrayal. He sought solace in the familiar embrace of Eddie (Vance) and Hattie, finding comfort in their unwavering support during this tumultuous time.

Amidst the chaos of his parents' divorce, Vance (Eddie) clung to the hope that someday, they would find healing and redemption. But for now, the wounds were raw, the pain palpable, as Vance (Eddie) and his family embarked on a journey of healing and rebuilding, one step at a time.

Vance (Eddie) approached her tentatively one evening, his heart heavy with the weight of their shared pain.

"Mom," he whispered softly, his voice barely audible above the gentle hum of the room.

Susan looked up, her eyes meeting Vance (Eddie)'s with a mixture of sorrow and gratitude. She offered him a weak smile, her lips trembling slightly as she beckoned him to sit beside her on the couch.

Vance (Eddie) hesitated for a moment before taking a seat, his hand reaching out to grasp Susan's in a silent gesture of support. They sat in silence for a while, the only sound being the quiet rhythm of their breathing.

Finally, Vance (Eddie) found the courage to speak, his voice filled with empathy and understanding. "I'm so sorry, Mom," he murmured, his words heavy with emotion. "I can't imagine how much you must be hurting right now."

Tears welled in Susan's eyes as she turned to look at her son, her heart aching with the pain of their shared sorrow. "Thank you, Vance," she whispered, her voice choked with emotion. "I never wanted you to see me like this."

Vance (Eddie) reached out, gently wiping away her tears with a tender touch. "You don't have to pretend to be strong, Mom," he said softly. "We're in this together, okay? Whatever you need, I'm here for you."

Susan nodded, her heart swelling with love and gratitude for her son. In that moment, as they sat together in the quiet comfort of their shared grief, Susan found solace in Vance (Eddie)'s unwavering support, knowing that no matter what the future held, they would face it together as a family.

The aftermath of the divorce sent shockwaves through Vance (Eddie)'s family, leaving them grappling with the harsh realities of betrayal and loss. As the dust settled, John made a decision that further deepened the wounds of their fractured family—he moved in with his mistress.

For Vance (Eddie), the news was a bitter pill to swallow, a painful reminder of the shattered dreams and broken promises that now defined his family's reality. He watched helplessly as his father's actions tore at the already fragile bonds that once held them together.

As John embarked on a new chapter of his life with his mistress, the chasm between father and son widened, leaving Vance (Eddie) feeling adrift in a sea of confusion and resentment. He struggled to reconcile the image of the man he once idolized with the harsh reality of his betrayal.

Despite his anger and disappointment, Vance (Eddie) couldn't shake the nagging feeling of sorrow that engulfed him, knowing that his family would never be the same again. He found solace in the unwavering support of his mother, Susan, who remained a pillar of strength amidst the chaos of their shattered lives.

But as Vance (Eddie) watched his father walk away, leaving behind a trail of broken promises and shattered dreams, he couldn't help but wonder if forgiveness was possible. In the midst of all this pain, he clung to the hope that someday, they would find healing and redemption. But for now, the wounds remained raw, and the scars were a painful reminder of the fractured family they had become.

Chapter 11

Four years had passed since Eddie (Vance) and Hattie started dating. In those years, their relationship had been a sanctuary, a haven away from the turmoil that plagued Eddie (Vance)'s family life. Hattie had been his rock, his confidante, his everything. Together, they had weathered storms, celebrated triumphs, and woven dreams of a future filled with love and happiness.

Yet, even amidst their own bliss, Eddie (Vance) couldn't escape the shadows of the events that had led to them being together. It was traumatizing for him. The pain lingered; it was like an ever-present weight on his shoulders. He often found himself grappling with conflicting emotions—love for his family, resentment for his father's choices, and a longing for the harmony they had lost.

As Eddie (Vance) reflected on the journey they had undertaken together, he realized how profoundly Hattie had shaped his understanding of forgiveness and resilience. Her unwavering belief in the power of love to heal wounds had been a guiding light through the darkest moments.

Despite the passage of time, Eddie (Vance) couldn't shake the nagging question that gnawed at his soul: could forgiveness bridge the chasm that divided his family? Was redemption possible, or were they destined to remain prisoners of their past?

Turning to Hattie, Eddie (Vance) sought solace in her comforting presence. She listened with empathy as he poured out his heart, his words a torrent of emotion that had long been suppressed.

"Hattie," Eddie (Vance) began, his voice trembling with vulnerability, "Do you believe in forgiveness? Do you think it's possible to mend what's broken, to find redemption even in the darkest of times?"

Hattie's eyes, pools of understanding, met his gaze. "Yes, Eddie," she said softly, her hand reaching out to touch his. "I believe that forgiveness is the key to healing. It's not easy, and it takes time. But with love and patience, anything is possible."

At that moment, Eddie (Vance) felt a glimmer of hope ignited within him. Perhaps forgiveness wasn't an unattainable ideal but a journey they could embark on together, hand in hand.

As the evening wore on, Eddie (Vance) and Hattie found themselves enveloped in a cocoon of love and understanding. In each other's arms, they found solace and strength, ready to face whatever challenges lay ahead.

Amidst the chaos of their shattered lives, a flicker of hope burned bright—a beacon of light guiding them toward a future where forgiveness, redemption, and love prevailed.

As the summer sun cast its golden glow over the landscape, Eddie (Vance) and Hattie embarked on what seemed like just another adventure — a road trip filled with laughter, shared dreams, and the promise of endless possibilities.

Their journey took them through winding roads and picturesque vistas, each mile bringing them closer together. Eddie (Vance) reveled in the freedom of the open road, the wind in his hair, and Hattie's laughter filling his heart with joy.

Throughout their travels, Eddie (Vance) remained blissfully unaware of the subtle changes in Hattie—a slight pallor to her complexion, a fleeting moment of fatigue in her eyes. He was too caught up in the magic of their shared moments to notice the shadows that danced at the edge of his vision.

Together, they explored quaint towns and hidden gems, their days filled with adventure and discovery. In the warmth of each other's company, Eddie (Vance) found solace from the chaos of the world, his heart singing with the joy of being alive.

As they watched the sun dip below the horizon, painting the sky in shades of orange and pink, Eddie (Vance) couldn't help but feel a sense of contentment wash over him. In that moment, surrounded by beauty and love, the future seemed limitless, filled with endless possibilities.

But unknown to Eddie (Vance), hidden beneath Hattie's radiant smile lay a secret—a truth she had chosen to keep buried deep within her heart. As they continued on their journey, each passing day brought them closer to a destination neither of them could foresee.

For Hattie, every moment with Eddie (Vance) was a precious gift—a chance to savor the sweetness of life before it slipped away. Though her heart ached with the weight of what was to come, she chose to cherish the present, holding onto the love they shared with every beat of her fragile heart.

And so, their road trip continued as a journey of love and discovery, unaware of the silent goodbye that lingered on the horizon. For Eddie (Vance)and Hattie, each moment together was a treasure—a memory to hold onto as they journeyed into the unknown.

As their road trip wound to a close, Eddie (Vance) and Hattie found themselves lost in conversation, their words a symphony of love and longing. In the quiet moments between laughter and shared dreams, Eddie (Vance) felt a sense of peace wash over him—a feeling of belonging that he had never known before.

As they returned home, Eddie (Vance) was filled with a renewed sense of purpose, his heart overflowing with gratitude for the love they shared. But little did he know, tragedy lurked just beyond the horizon, waiting to shatter the fragile illusion of happiness they had built together.

One fateful day, as Vance toiled away at work, a sudden sense of unease gripped his heart—a foreboding whisper that something was terribly wrong. Ignoring the nagging feeling in the pit of his stomach, Eddie (Vance) focused on his tasks, oblivious to the tragedy unfolding miles away.

Meanwhile, at home, Hattie's smile faded as a sharp pain pierced her chest—a silent scream that echoed through the empty rooms of their once vibrant home. With every beat of her failing heart, Hattie's strength waned, her breaths growing shallow as she fought to hold onto life with every ounce of her being.

Alone and frightened, Hattie reached for the phone, her trembling fingers dialing Eddie (Vance)'s number in a desperate bid for help. But fate had other plans, and as the seconds ticked by, Hattie's strength began to fade, her world slipping away into darkness.

By the time Vance received the call, it was too late—a cruel twist of fate that left him reeling with shock and disbelief. Racing home with a heart heavy with sorrow, Eddie (Vance) prayed for a miracle—a chance to hold Hattie in his arms once more and tell her how much she meant to him.

But as he arrived at their doorstep, Eddie (Vance)'s worst fears were realized—a scene of devastation that shattered his world into a million jagged pieces. For there, lying on the cold tile floor, was Hattie—her eyes closed in eternal slumber, her spirit soaring free from the pain that had plagued her weary soul.

At that moment, Vance's heart broke in two—a gaping chasm of grief and regret that threatened to swallow him whole. As he knelt beside Hattie's lifeless form, tears streaming down his cheeks, Vance whispered words of love and longing into the silent void—a final farewell to the woman who had stolen his heart and changed his life forever.

And as the world continued to spin, oblivious to the tragedy that had unfolded within its midst, Eddie (Vance) clung to the memories of their time together—a beacon of light in the darkness, guiding him through the storm that raged within his shattered soul.

In the days that followed Hattie's sudden passing, Eddie (Vance) found himself navigating a blur of grief and disbelief—a world devoid of color and warmth, where every breath felt like a burden too heavy to bear.

As he stood beside Hattie's casket, surrounded by family and friends gathered to pay their final respects, Eddie (Vance) felt a crushing weight settle over him—a suffocating blanket of sorrow that threatened to consume him whole.

The sight of Hattie lying motionless in her casket was a dagger to Eddie (Vance)'s heart—a visceral reminder of the vibrant spirit that had been extinguished far too soon. Her once luminous eyes were closed forever, her laughter silenced by the cruel hand of fate.

As Eddie (Vance) gazed upon her still form, a torrent of emotions threatened to overwhelm him—anger, regret, and a tremendous sense of loss that threatened to consume him whole. He wanted to scream, to rail against the unfairness of it all, but his voice was lost in the sea of mournful whispers that filled the air.

At that moment, surrounded by the hushed solemnity of the funeral parlor, Eddie (Vance) felt utterly alone—a solitary figure adrift in a sea of sorrow. And as he clung to the memories of their time together, he vowed to honor Hattie's memory in any way he could—to live each day with the same passion and zest for life that she had embodied so effortlessly.

As the funeral procession made its way to the cemetery, Eddie (Vance) followed in a daze, his steps heavy with the weight of his grief. The world seemed to move in slow motion around him, each moment stretching into eternity as he grappled with the reality of Hattie's absence.

And as they laid Hattie to rest beneath a blanket of earth and sky, Eddie (Vance) felt a part of himself go with her—a piece of his heart forever entwined with hers in the silent embrace of eternity. But amidst the pain and sorrow, Eddie (Vance) found solace in the knowledge that Hattie's spirit would live on in the hearts of those who loved her—a beacon of light guiding them through the darkest of nights.

***

In the days and weeks that followed Hattie's funeral, Eddie (Vance) found himself grappling with a profound sense of emptiness—a void that no amount of time or tears could ever hope to fill. Everywhere he turned, he was haunted by memories of their time together—their laughter, their dreams, the whispered promises of a future that would never come to pass.

But amidst the pain and sorrow, Eddie (Vance) made a decision—a choice born of both necessity and self-preservation. He resolved to stay single, to forgo the pursuit of love in favor of honoring Hattie's memory and safeguarding his own fragile heart.

For Eddie (Vance), the thought of opening himself up to the possibility of love once more felt like an impossible feat—a betrayal of the love he had shared with Hattie, a rejection of the life they had dreamed of together. The wounds were still too raw, the pain too fresh, for Eddie (Vance) to even entertain the idea of moving on.

So, he threw himself into his work, immersing himself in the familiar rhythms of routine in a desperate bid to distract himself from the ache that gnawed at his soul. But try as he might to bury his grief beneath a facade of busyness, Eddie (Vance) could not escape the echoes of Hattie's laughter, the ghost of her presence that lingered in every corner of their once-shared home.

In the quiet moments of solitude, Eddie (Vance) found himself reflecting on the nature of love and loss—the fragile threads that bound them together, the inevitability of their eventual unraveling. He realized that to love was to invite pain, to open oneself up to the possibility of heartbreak and disappointment—a risk he was no longer willing to take.

And so, Eddie (Vance) made peace with his decision—a solemn vow to cherish the memories of his time with Hattie, to live each day with purpose and gratitude in her honor. Though his heart may never fully heal from the wounds of her absence, Eddie (Vance) found solace in the knowledge that their love would endure—a beacon of light guiding him through the darkest of nights, a reminder that even in death, Hattie's spirit would always be by his side.

***

Despite Eddie (Vance)'s resolve to remain single in the wake of Hattie's passing, the weight of his grief only seemed to grow heavier with each passing day. The laughter that once filled his home had long since faded into silence, replaced by a profound sense of loneliness that gnawed at his soul.

Vance (Eddie), seeing his friend's struggle, couldn't bear to watch Eddie (Vance) suffer in silence any longer. With a heavy heart and a determination born of love, Vance (Eddie) approached Eddie (Vance) one evening, his concern etched upon his face.

"Eddie (Vance)," Vance (Eddie) began gently, "I can see that something has been troubling you. I hate to see you like this. You can't keep shutting yourself off from the world forever. You deserve to find happiness again."

Eddie (Vance), caught off guard by Vance (Eddie)'s words, felt a surge of resistance well up within him. He couldn't tell his friend what he was going through, for he never revealed his relationship with Hattie to the world. The thought of moving on, of opening his heart to another, felt like a betrayal of the love he had shared with Hattie—a wound too deep to ever fully heal.

But Vance (Eddie), ever the voice of reason, refused to be swayed by Eddie (Vance)'s protests. With a mixture of patience and persistence, he gently encouraged Eddie (Vance) to consider the possibility of dating.

At first, Eddie (Vance) recoiled at the suggestion, his heart still raw from the loss he had endured. But as Vance (Eddie) spoke of the importance of healing and moving forward, Eddie (Vance) couldn't help but feel a flicker of hope ignite within him—a tiny spark of possibility amidst the darkness that threatened to consume him whole.

With Vance (Eddie)'s unwavering support and encouragement, Eddie (Vance) tentatively dipped his toe back into the waters of the dating world—a hesitant step toward a future that felt both terrifying and exhilarating in equal measure.

As he navigated the uncertain terrain of love and loss once more, Eddie (Vance) found solace in the knowledge that he was not alone—that no matter what the future held, he would always have Vance (Eddie) by his side, a constant source of strength and support in times of need. And though the road ahead may be fraught with challenges and obstacles, Eddie (Vance) knew that with Vance (Eddie) by his side, he would never have to face them alone.

Reluctantly, Eddie (Vance) allowed Vance (Eddie) to create an online dating profile for him. With a mix of trepidation and curiosity, Eddie (Vance) tentatively dipped his toes into the digital dating pool, unsure of what to expect but willing to give it a try.

As his profile went live, Eddie (Vance) found himself inundated with messages and requests from women eager to get to know him. Each interaction brought with it a mix of excitement and apprehension as Eddie (Vance) navigated the complexities of online dating with cautious optimism.

Over the next year and a half, Eddie (Vance) went on numerous dates with women he met through the online platform. Some were fleeting encounters, little more than coffee dates or casual dinners, while others blossomed into short-lived flings that fizzled out as quickly as they began.

Through it all, Eddie (Vance) kept things casual, wary of investing too much of himself in any one relationship. He was still grappling with the lingering pain of Hattie's passing, and the thought of opening his heart to someone new felt like a daunting task—one he wasn't quite ready to undertake.

Yet, amidst the string of casual encounters, Eddie (Vance) found moments of genuine connection and companionship. He shared laughter and conversation with his dates, finding solace in their company even as he kept them at arm's length.

Through these experiences, Eddie (Vance) learned valuable lessons about himself and what he truly wanted in a partner. He discovered that while casual dating provided a temporary distraction from his grief, it was ultimately companionship and connection that he craved—a depth of emotional intimacy that transcended the superficiality of fleeting encounters.

And though his journey through the world of online dating was far from perfect, Eddie (Vance) emerged from the experience with a newfound sense of clarity and purpose. He realized that while Hattie would always hold a special place in his heart, he was capable of opening himself up to love once more—to embrace the possibility of finding happiness in unexpected places.

Eddie (Vance) also found solace in the comforting embrace of family and friends. Despite the challenges he faced, he made a conscious effort to nurture his relationships and cherish the moments spent with those he held dear.

With Vance (Eddie) by his side, Eddie (Vance) embarked on countless adventures and shared countless laughs, their brotherly bond serving as a source of strength and support in times of need. Whether it was a weekend hiking trip in the mountains or a quiet evening at home reminiscing about old times, Eddie (Vance) cherished every moment spent in Vance (Eddie)'s company, grateful for the unwavering love and companionship they shared.

Eddie (Vance) found solace in the company of his family, who stood by him through the highs and lows of his journey. He cherished the Sunday dinners and holiday gatherings spent surrounded by loved ones, the laughter and camaraderie serving as a balm for his wounded soul.

And then there were his friends—loyal companions who had been by his side through thick and thin. From childhood buddies to college pals, Eddie (Vance)surrounded himself with a tight-knit circle of confidants who provided a much-needed sense of normalcy amidst the chaos of his life.

Together, they shared countless memories and inside jokes, supporting each other through life's trials and tribulations with unwavering loyalty and affection. Whether it was a spontaneous road trip or a quiet night playing board games, Eddie (Vance) cherished the bond he shared with his friends, knowing that they were always there for him no matter what.

In their company, Eddie (Vance) found moments of joy and laughter amidst the pain and sorrow—a reminder that even in the darkest of times, there was light to be found in the love and companionship of those who mattered most.

And so, as Eddie (Vance) continued to navigate the winding road of life, he took comfort in the knowledge that no matter what the future held, he was surrounded by a supportive network of family and friends who would walk beside him every step of the way. And in their love and companionship, Eddie (Vance) found the strength to face whatever challenges lay ahead, knowing that he was never truly alone.

Chapter 12

The sun hung low in the sky, casting a warm golden glow over Susan's backyard as she prepared for her annual 4th of July barbecue party. Colorful bunting fluttered in the gentle breeze, strung between sturdy wooden posts, adding a festive touch to the scene. The air was filled with the mouthwatering aroma of sizzling burgers and hot dogs on the grill, mingling with the sweet scent of freshly cut grass.

Vance (Eddie) watched from the edge of the bustling gathering with a wide smile on his face, his heart swelling with joy at the sight of his mother, Susan, laughing and chatting animatedly with their friends and neighbors. It had been a while since he had seen her so carefree and happy, and the sight warmed his heart more than he could express.

As guests began to arrive, laughter and chatter filled the air, blending seamlessly with the upbeat tunes emanating from the speakers strategically placed around the yard. Children darted around playing games of tag and tossing a frisbee, their gleeful shrieks adding to the lively atmosphere.

The backyard was transformed into a patchwork of picnic blankets and lawn chairs, each occupied by friends and family eagerly catching up and sharing stories. In one corner, a group of friends clustered around a makeshift bar, clinking glasses of chilled lemonade or frosty beers as they toasted to the holiday and the bonds that brought them together.

The tantalizing aroma of barbecue drew a crowd of hungry revelers to the grill, where Susan and a few friends tended to the sizzling fare with practiced expertise. Burgers sizzled and popped, sending up clouds of savory smoke that mingled with the scent of charred meat and caramelized onions.

Vance (Eddie) couldn't help but feel a swell of happiness as he moved through the crowd, exchanging hugs and hearty handshakes with familiar faces. But it was the sight of his mother, her face radiant with joy as she moved effortlessly among their guests, that filled him with the most profound sense of contentment.

Soon enough, the sun dipped lower on the horizon, casting long shadows across the lawn. Susan called everyone to gather around for the main event: a spectacular fireworks display. Cheers erupted as colorful bursts of light illuminated the night sky, painting dazzling patterns against the darkness.

At that moment, as Vance (Eddie) watched the fireworks dance and sparkle overhead, he felt a profound sense of gratitude wash over him. Here, surrounded by the people he loved most in the world and seeing his mother so happy, he knew that no matter what challenges lay ahead, he would always find strength and support in their unwavering friendship and love.

***

As the last echoes of the fireworks faded into the night, Eddie (Vance) found himself drawn to Susan, a quiet resolve in his heart to share his burdens with her. He approached Susan, who was now sitting on a cozy bench beneath the twinkling lights strung from tree branches above.

"Susan," he began softly, "I've been meaning to talk to you about something."

Susan turned to him, her expression gentle and attentive. "Of course, sweetheart. What's on your mind?"

Eddie (Vance) took a deep breath, the weight of recent losses heavy on his shoulders. "I've been struggling lately," he admitted, his voice tinged with vulnerability. "You know, work, personal life, it has all hit rock bottom."

Susan reached out, placing a comforting hand on his arm. "I'm so sorry, Eddie (Vance)," she murmured, her eyes filled with empathy. "Whatever else you're going through, you don't have to face it alone."

Tears pricked at the corners of Eddie (Vance)'s eyes as he leaned into Susan's reassuring touch. "Thank you, Susan," he whispered, the weight on his heart easing ever so slightly. "It means everything to me to have you here."

As they sat together in companionable silence, Susan took a deep breath, her own struggles weighing heavily on her mind. "How have you been holding up?" Eddie (Vance) asked.

"It's been tough," she admitted, her voice catching in her throat. " John's betrayal hit me harder than I thought it would."

Eddie (Vance) listened with a sympathetic ear as Susan poured out her heart, his presence a steady anchor in the storm of his emotions. Together, they navigated the choppy waters of grief and sorrow, finding solace and strength in each other's unwavering support.

In that moment, as they shared their pain and sorrow with each other, Vance (Eddie) and Susan found a deep and profound connection that transcended words. In the warmth of each other's embrace, they found comfort and solace, knowing that no matter what life threw their way, they would always have each other to lean on.

***

As the lively chatter of the barbecue gradually subsided and the last embers of the grill cooled, Eddie (Vance) and Susan found themselves seated at the now-empty picnic table, their conversation taking a more somber turn. The glow of the string lights above cast a soft illumination over their faces as they spoke about the recent losses they had endured.

The weight of grief hung heavy in the air, yet amidst the sorrow, there was a palpable sense of closeness and connection between mother and son. In each other's presence, they found solace and strength, drawing comfort from the shared understanding of their pain.

The night grew late, and the guests began to bid their farewells. Susan's cheeks flushed with the effects of one too many glasses of wine. Eddie (Vance) gently guided her to her feet, offering his arm for support as they made their way to the kitchen.

"Let me take care of this," Eddie (Vance) insisted, his voice tender with affection. "You've done enough today."

Susan smiled gratefully, her exhaustion evident in the lines of her face. "Thank you, sweetheart," she murmured, leaning heavily against him. "I don't know what I'd do without you."

Together, they worked in companionable silence, the clatter of dishes and the rush of running water filling the air. As Vance

(Eddie) scrubbed away the remnants of the evening's feast, he couldn't help but feel a swell of gratitude for the opportunity to care for his mother in her time of need.

With each plate washed and dried, the burden on their hearts grew a little lighter, the act of tending to the mundane tasks of everyday life offering a small reprieve from the weight of their grief.

***

As Eddie (Vance) tiptoed towards the door, intending to slip away quietly before Susan's inebriated state became too much to handle, Susan's voice called out from behind him, her tone laced with a playful insistence.

"Leaving already, sweetheart?" she slurred slightly, her words carrying a hint of mischief.

Eddie (Vance) froze in his tracks, turning to find Susan swaying slightly in the doorway, a mischievous glint in her eyes. Despite her inebriation, there was a playful energy about her that was hard to resist.

"I was just going to say goodnight, Susan," Eddie (Vance) replied, trying to mask his discomfort with a gentle smile. "You've had a long day, and I don't want to keep you up."

But Susan waved away his concerns with a careless flick of her hand, her movements exaggerated by the effects of the alcohol. "Nonsense, sweetheart! The night is still young, and I'm not ready to say goodbye just yet."

Before Eddie (Vance) could protest further, Susan grabbed his hand and tugged him back into the living room, her laughter ringing out like music in the quiet night.

"Come on, Vance!" she exclaimed, her voice bubbly with excitement. "Let's have one more drink together. Just you and me, celebrating life and all its little joys."

Caught off guard by Susan's unexpected enthusiasm, Eddie (Vance) found himself unable to resist her infectious spirit. With a resigned sigh, he sank onto the couch beside her, the weight of the day melting away in the warmth of her laughter.

For hours, they talked and laughed, sharing stories and memories as the night stretched on around them. As the first light of dawn began to filter through the windows, Eddie (Vance) realized with a start that he had never felt more alive than in that moment, surrounded by the love and laughter of his dear friend.

In the soft glow of the morning light, Susan leaned in close, her gaze lingering on Eddie (Vance)'s face with an intensity that sent a shiver down his spine. "Thank you, Eddie," she whispered, her voice husky with emotion. "For being here, for being you. I don't know what I'd do without you."

At that moment, Eddie (Vance) knew that he would always be there for Susan through the highs and lows of life, come what may. For in her laughter and tears, he had found a kindred spirit, a friend whose love and companionship would light his way through even the darkest nights.

In a moment of heated passion, their lips met in a desperate kiss, igniting a fire that burned hot and fierce between them. Clothes were discarded with abandon as they surrendered to the undeniable pull of their mutual longing, their bodies entwined in a tangle of limbs and whispered promises.

In the aftermath, as the soft rays of sun filtered through the curtains, Susan's expression turned somber, her eyes clouded with uncertainty and regret. "I'm sorry, Eddie," she murmured, her voice tinged with sadness. "I didn't mean for this to happen."

But Eddie (Vance) reached out, gently brushing a stray lock of hair from her face. "It's okay, Susan," he whispered, his own heart heavy with conflicting emotions. "We're in this together, whatever it may be."

Despite their initial misgivings, the spark between them refused to be extinguished, drawing them back into each other's arms time and time again. What had begun as a fleeting moment of passion soon blossomed into a secret relationship, hidden from prying eyes behind closed doors and whispered promises.

Their encounters became clandestine meetings, stolen moments of passion amidst the chaos of their everyday lives. And though they both knew the risks of their forbidden love, they couldn't deny the pull of their shared desire, the need for each other growing stronger with each passing day.

But as the days turned into weeks and the weeks into months, the weight of their secret began to take its toll. Guilt and shame gnawed at Susan's conscience, while Eddie (Vance) found himself torn between his love for Susan and the fear of what their relationship might cost them both.

Yet despite the odds stacked against them, they couldn't seem to stay away from each other, drawn together by a love that defied logic and reason. And so, they continued to walk the precarious tightrope of their forbidden romance, clinging to each other in the face of a world that they would never understand.

Chapter 13

A future with Eddie (Vance), acknowledged and celebrated by her family, had felt like a shimmering mirage to Susan. It was a fantasy whispered in stolen glances and hushed conversations, a world so far removed from their clandestine meetings. Yet, fate, that capricious trickster, had a different script in mind. A stroke of unexpected fortune, a twist in the grand narrative of life, brought them together once more. Not in the hushed corners of stolen moments but bathed in the warm glow of a family barbecue, a scene straight out of a life Susan could only dream of.

Susan's initial trepidation, a knot of apprehension tightening in her stomach, loosened its grip as she witnessed Eddie (Vance) approach her. He carried a plate heaped high with potato salad. A nervous grin was stretched a little too wide across his face. Yet, the awkwardness was endearing. The conversation, to her surprise, flowed with an unexpected ease. Eddie (Vance)'s inherent charm, like a secret weapon, disarmed even her stoic oldest brother.

He spoke of his work with a passion that crackled in the air, contagious and enthralling. As Susan listened, she saw him in a new light. He wasn't just the object of her forbidden desires, a stolen piece of happiness. He was a man with dreams and aspirations that mirrored her own, a kindred spirit she could connect with on a deeper level. This revelation, unexpected and profound, sent a warmth blossoming in her chest, a warmth that rivaled the golden light of the setting sun.

Later, as the sun dipped below the horizon, casting long shadows across the lawn, Susan found herself alone with Eddie (Vance) by the old oak tree, a silent witness to countless childhood memories. He spoke softly, his voice laced with a newfound honesty. He confessed his past feelings, the reasons for their clandestine meetings, and the guilt that had gnawed at him ever since.

Susan listened, her heart a tangled mess of emotions. Relief warred with a tinge of anger at his initial deception. Yet, as he spoke of the fear of rejection, of losing her altogether, a sliver of understanding bloomed within her.

Taking a deep breath, Susan shared her own fears, the burden of defying her family's expectations. But as she looked into Eddie (Vance)'s hopeful eyes, a newfound determination took root within her. Maybe, just maybe, there was another way.

With trembling hands, she reached out and grasped his. "Let's try this the right way," she whispered, her voice thick with emotion. Eddie (Vance)'s face broke into a radiant smile, a silent promise hanging heavy in the twilight air.

It wasn't a fairy tale. There were whispers and judging stares to endure, bridges to rebuild and trust to re-earn. But with the weight of secrecy lifted, Susan and Vance embarked on a new chapter, their love story finally bathed in the warm light of acceptance.

A new storm brewed on the horizon – her son, Vance (Eddie). Unlike his initial acceptance, Eddie remained stubbornly aloof. Eddie (Vance) tried everything, but Vance (Eddie) remained distant, his disapproval a dark cloud hanging over their newfound happiness.

Susan suspected it stemmed from a deeper, more unsettling place. Vance (Eddie) and Eddie (Vance) had known each other ever since high school. In Vance (Eddie)'s eyes, their relationship transcended a betrayal of his trust; it was a violation of a boundary, something deeply personal and uncomfortable. Susan tried talking to Vance (Eddie), explaining the complexities of her feelings for Eddie (Vance), the guilt that gnawed at her, and ultimately, the decision to come clean. But Vance (Eddie) remained unconvinced. He saw Eddie (Vance) not just as an interloper but as someone who had crossed a line, blurring the already complicated dynamic of their family unit.

Eddie (Vance), on the other hand, remained unfazed by Vance (Eddie)'s icy demeanor. He understood his friend's shock, the need to adjust to a completely unexpected reality. Eddie (Vance) wasn't about to force himself into Vance (Eddie)'s life or their relationship with this new identity as his mom’s partner. He focused his energy on Susan, building a foundation of trust and love. He helped her navigate the emotional rollercoaster of dealing with Vance (Eddie), offering unwavering support and a shoulder to cry on.

Meanwhile, another life-altering event unfolded. Susan decided to sell her house. Eddie (Vance), however, saw it as an opportunity. He suggested they use the money Susan received from the sale as a down payment on a new place – a fresh start, a home they could build together.

Susan was hesitant at first. The idea of leaving behind the familiar comfort of her childhood neighborhood was daunting. But seeing Eddie (Vance)'s unwavering enthusiasm and his genuine desire to create a future with her, a future that included even Vance (Eddie), she finally relented. They found a charming little cottage on the outskirts of town with a sprawling backyard that promised endless possibilities for rebuilding connections.

Moving day arrived, a bittersweet symphony of packing boxes and tearful goodbyes. As Susan stood on Hattie's porch one last time, she glanced at Eddie (Vance), his hand resting reassuringly on her shoulder. There was a flicker of sadness in his eyes, a silent acknowledgment of the memories left behind. But as their gazes met, a brighter emotion shone through – hope. Hope for a future built on love, acceptance, and maybe, just maybe, even Vance (Eddie) coming around.

The bittersweet pang of leaving Hattie's house lingered long after the moving truck rumbled away. Susan, despite the excitement of a new beginning with Eddie (Vance), couldn't help but steal glances back at the empty Victorian, a silent goodbye to a lifetime of memories. Eddie (Vance), ever perceptive, squeezed her hand reassuringly.

"We'll make new memories, love," he murmured, his voice filled with an unwavering optimism that warmed her heart.

Meanwhile, unbeknownst to Eddie (Vance), a small package arrived at his doorstep a few days later. It was addressed in Hattie's elegant script, a stark contrast to the worn cardboard box. Inside, nestled amongst faded photographs and a hand-stitched quilt, was a crisp envelope. Curiosity piqued, Eddie

(Vance) opened it to find a letter and a hefty stack of bills. Hattie, in her characteristically no-nonsense way, had expressed her gratitude for his kindness and companionship over the years. The envelope contained a sum of money – a staggering $25,000 – a token of her appreciation for the unwavering support he'd shown her.

Eddie (Vance) stared at the money, a mix of emotions swirling within him. He felt a surge of gratitude for Hattie's generosity, a testament to the deep bond they'd shared. But a flicker of unease shadowed his joy. There was a chance that Susan, who was still struggling with Vance (Eddie)'s disapproval, might misinterpret the money. He knew she wouldn't be comfortable with him keeping such a large sum, especially considering the unconventional beginnings of their relationship.

Later that evening, after Vance (Eddie) had retreated to his room, Eddie (Vance) brought up the envelope. He explained everything – Hattie's letter, the money, and his concerns. Susan listened intently, her initial surprise melting into a warm understanding.

"It's mom's way of looking out for you," Susan said gently, taking his hand. "She knew you wouldn't ask for anything, but she wanted to show her appreciation."

A thoughtful silence descended upon them. The weight of the money, both literal and metaphorical, hung heavy in the air. Finally, Susan spoke again, her voice filled with determination.

"We can use it for the house," she suggested. "A down payment on renovations, maybe even that pool you've always wanted in the backyard. It could be a way to honor mom's memory, a way to create a space where we can all feel comfortable, even Vance (Eddie)."

Eddie (Vance)'s face broke into a smile. Susan's suggestion not only addressed his concerns but also offered a potential solution to the ever-present tension with Vance (Eddie). A backyard pool – a neutral ground, a chance to bond over shared summer afternoons – it was a long shot, but a hopeful one nonetheless.

The next day, they sat down together and pored over house plans, their laughter echoing through the empty rooms. The future, once uncertain, now shimmered with possibility. The money from Hattie became a symbol – not just of her generosity but of the hope for a new beginning. It was a chance to build a home not just of bricks and mortar but of love, acceptance, and maybe, just maybe, even a begrudging friendship between a son and his mother's new love.

Chapter 14

The sun peeked through the curtains, gently nudging Eddie (Vance) awake. With a contented sigh, he stretched his arms above his head, relishing in the warmth of the morning light filtering into their bedroom.

Rolling over, Eddie (Vance) reached for Susan, finding her already awake and scrolling through her phone, a cup of coffee steaming on the bedside table.

"Morning, love," Eddie (Vance) greeted, planting a soft kiss on her cheek.

"Morning, sleepyhead," Susan replied with a smile, setting her phone aside. "Coffee's ready whenever you are."

With a grateful nod, Eddie (Vance) swung his legs over the edge of the bed and padded into the kitchen, where the aroma of freshly brewed coffee enveloped him. He poured himself a mug, savoring the rich flavor as he leaned against the countertop.

Their morning routine was simple yet comforting. Eddie (Vance) worked as a nurse at the hospital nearby, his shifts varying but always filled with the hum of activity and the satisfaction of making a difference in people's lives. Susan, on the other hand, worked remotely as a freelance graphic designer, allowing her the flexibility to manage her own schedule.

Despite their busy lives, they always made time for each other. Whether it was sharing breakfast together before Eddie (Vance)'s early morning shift or cuddling on the couch after a long day, their bond only seemed to grow stronger with each passing moment.

As Eddie (Vance) finished his coffee, he glanced out the window, the sight of their backyard sparking a flicker of excitement within him. Plans for renovations and a new pool danced in his mind, a tangible symbol of their future together.

Turning to Susan, Eddie (Vance) couldn't help but smile. "You know, I can't wait to start working on the house. It's going to be amazing."

Susan returned his smile, her eyes sparkling with enthusiasm. "I know, right? I can already picture it – our little slice of paradise."

With a shared glance filled with hope and determination, Eddie (Vance) and Susan knew that their journey was just beginning. As they embraced each other, the possibilities of the future stretched out before them, filled with endless potential and boundless love.

Weeks passed in a whirlwind of anticipation and excitement as Eddie (Vance) and Susan dove headfirst into their plans for the house renovations. Each day brought new decisions to be made, from selecting paint colors to debating the layout of the backyard pool.

Amidst the chaos of hammering and drilling, Eddie (Vance) found himself increasingly grateful for the love and support of Susan by his side. She was his rock, his confidante, and his partner in every sense of the word.

One balmy evening, as they sat on the porch sipping lemonade after a long day of work, Eddie (Vance) felt a surge of nervous energy course through him. The time had come to take the next step in their journey together.

Clearing his throat, Eddie (Vance) reached for Susan's hand, his heart pounding in his chest. "Susan, there's something I want to ask you."

Susan turned to him, her eyes filled with curiosity and affection. "What is it, Eddie (Vance)?"

Taking a deep breath, Eddie (Vance) locked eyes with Susan, his voice steady despite the flutter of butterflies in his stomach. "I love you more than words can express, and I can't imagine spending my life with anyone else. Susan, will you marry me?"

For a moment, time seemed to stand still as Susan processed Eddie (Vance)'s words. Then, a radiant smile spread across her face, her eyes shimmering with tears of joy.

"Yes, Eddie! A thousand times yes!" Susan exclaimed, throwing her arms around him in a tight embrace.

As Eddie (Vance) slipped the ring onto Susan's finger, the weight of his love and commitment settled over them like a warm embrace. In that moment, surrounded by the echoes of their laughter and the promise of their future together, Eddie (Vance) knew that he had found his forever home in Susan's heart.

***

With the excitement of their engagement still lingering in the air, Eddie (Vance) and Susan dove headfirst into the whirlwind of wedding preparations. From choosing the perfect venue to selecting flowers and invitations, every detail was meticulously planned with love and care.

As they poured over wedding magazines and scrolled through Pinterest boards, Eddie (Vance) couldn't help but marvel at the depth of Susan's love and commitment. She approached each task with a sense of joy and enthusiasm that was infectious, and Eddie (Vance) found himself falling more deeply in love with her with each passing day.

Amidst the flurry of activity, however, Eddie (Vance) couldn't shake the feeling of apprehension regarding Vance (Eddie). While their relationship had improved since Eddie (Vance) and Susan moved in together, there was still a lingering tension between them – a silent understanding of the divide that existed between the two best friends.

Despite his reservations, Eddie (Vance) was determined to bridge the gap and forge a bond with Eddie built on mutual respect and understanding. He knew that winning Vance (Eddie)'s acceptance was crucial not only for their relationship but for the harmony of their new family.

Slowly but surely, Eddie (Vance) began to involve Vance (Eddie) in the wedding preparations, seeking his input on everything from the music playlist to the menu selection. At first, Vance (Eddie) remained aloof and guarded, his skepticism apparent in his terse responses and reluctant participation.

However, as the days turned into weeks and Eddie (Vance) continued to extend an olive branch, Vance (Eddie)'s demeanor began to soften. He watched with quiet curiosity as Eddie (Vance) and Susan navigated the challenges of wedding planning together, their love and commitment shining through even in the face of adversity.

Gradually, Vance (Eddie)'s walls began to crumble, replaced by a newfound sense of acceptance and understanding. He realized that Eddie (Vance) wasn't trying to replace his father or erase his memory – he was simply embracing the love and happiness that Susan deserved.

On the eve of the wedding, as Eddie (Vance) stood before Vance (Eddie) in his sharp suit, a nervous smile playing on his lips, Vance (Eddie) extended his hand in a gesture of friendship and acceptance.

"I may not always understand your relationship with my mom, but I can see how much you love her," Vance (Eddie) said quietly, his eyes reflecting a mixture of vulnerability and sincerity. "And that's all that matters to me."

Touched by Vance (Eddie)'s words, Eddie (Vance) felt a surge of gratitude and relief wash over him. At that moment, surrounded by the love and support of their family and friends, Eddie (Vance) knew that their journey was just beginning – a journey filled with love, acceptance, and the promise of a brighter future together. This, however, wasn't their happily ever after, as fate had more happiness and trials in store for them.

Eddie (Vance) and Susan began their married life on a good note. The first year went by in marital bliss. As the second year of their marriage dawned, Eddie (Vance) and Susan found themselves embracing the joyous anticipation of expanding their family. Their love had blossomed into something beautiful and enduring, and now they eagerly awaited the arrival of their first child together.

When Susan finally gave birth to their daughter, Megan, their hearts overflowed with love and gratitude. She was a radiant bundle of joy, her laughter filling their home with warmth and light.

A decade later, just as their happiness seemed boundless, a dark cloud descended upon their lives. Susan began to experience inexplicable bouts of fatigue and nausea, her once vibrant energy dimming with each passing day.

Concerned for her well-being, Eddie (Vance) urged Susan to see a doctor, but she brushed off his concerns, attributing her symptoms to stress and fatigue. However, as weeks turned into months and her condition failed to improve, Susan could no longer ignore the persistent ache in her abdomen and the gnawing sense of unease that plagued her.

Reluctantly, Susan agreed to undergo a series of tests, her heart heavy with fear and uncertainty. And when the results came back, their worst fears were realized – Susan had been diagnosed with pancreatic cancer.

The news struck like a thunderbolt, leaving Eddie (Vance) and Susan reeling in disbelief. How could something so cruel and unfathomable threaten to tear apart the life they had worked so hard to build?

In the days that followed, Eddie (Vance) stood by Susan's side as she underwent grueling rounds of chemotherapy and radiation, his love and support unwavering in the face of adversity. Together, they clung to hope, drawing strength from each other's presence as they navigated the uncertain terrain of Susan's illness.

But as months passed and Susan's condition worsened, their hope began to wane. Despite the best efforts of her medical team and the unwavering support of their loved ones, the cancer continued to spread, leaving Eddie (Vance) and Susan grappling with the harsh reality of their mortality.

And as they faced the inevitable with courage and grace, Eddie (Vance) found solace in the memories they had created together – the laughter, the love, the moments of pure joy that had illuminated their lives like stars in the darkest of nights.

In the end, it was love that sustained them – love that transcended time and space, love that endured even in the face of death. During Susan's chemotherapy treatments, Eddie (Vance) became her unwavering pillar of support. He was there by her side through every appointment, holding her hand through the nausea and weakness that followed each session. He cooked her favorite meals, adjusted his work schedule to be with her whenever she needed him, and never once faltered in his commitment to her well-being.

As the toxic chemicals coursed through Susan's veins, Eddie (Vance) did everything in his power to ease her discomfort and alleviate her pain. He learned to anticipate her needs before she even had to ask, providing comfort and reassurance with a gentle touch or a loving embrace.

But as the cancer relentlessly progressed, Eddie (Vance)'s heart broke to see Susan's once vibrant spirit gradually fade away. No amount of love or care could stem the tide of her illness, and with each passing day, Eddie (Vance) felt the weight of their shared sorrow grow heavier upon his shoulders.

On Susan's last day, as they sat together in the quiet sanctuary of their home, Eddie (Vance) knew that their time together was drawing to a close. He held her frail form in his arms, his tears mingling with hers as they whispered words of love and longing.

In their final conversation, Susan's voice was weak but filled with a quiet resolve. She spoke of the pain and trauma she had endured in her youth, recounting the harrowing details of the assault that had left scars both seen and unseen.

With tears streaming down his face, Eddie (Vance) listened in stunned silence as Susan made her final request. She asked him to make a vow – a promise to seek justice for the innocent child she once was, to find the man responsible for shattering her innocence and robbing her of her peace.

At that moment, Eddie (Vance) felt a fire ignite within him – a burning determination to honor Susan's memory and fulfill her final wish. And as Susan took her final breath, surrounded by the love of her family, Eddie (Vance) knew that her legacy would live on in the hearts of those she left behind – a testament to the enduring power of love in the face of life's greatest challenges.

***

In the days that followed Susan's passing, Eddie (Vance) found himself navigating the hazy blur of grief and mourning with a heavy heart. Together with their family and friends, he meticulously planned a funeral and vigil to honor Susan's memory and celebrate the beautiful life she had lived.

The funeral was a somber affair, filled with tears and heartfelt eulogies that paid tribute to Susan's kindness, compassion, and unwavering strength. Friends and loved ones gathered to share stories and memories, finding solace in each other's presence as they mourned the loss of a beloved wife, mother, and friend.

Amidst the sea of mourners, Eddie (Vance) couldn't help but notice Vance (Eddie) standing off to the side, his expression a mask of grief and disbelief. Despite their tumultuous history, Eddie (Vance) could see the pain etched in Vance (Eddie)'s features – a silent testament to the depth of his love for Susan and the profound impact she had made on his life.

As the vigil drew to a close, Vance (Eddie) approached Eddie (Vance), his heart heavy with empathy and understanding. He reached out a hand in a gesture of solidarity, offering a silent comfort that transcended words.

"I'm so sorry, Eddie," Vance (Eddie) murmured, his voice thick with emotion. "I know how much she meant to you."

Eddie (Vance) met Vance (Eddie)'s gaze with a mixture of sadness and gratitude, his walls momentarily crumbling in the face of their shared loss. In that moment of vulnerability, Eddie (Vance) saw a glimpse of the boy he had once been – a boy who had loved Susan with all his heart despite the pain and resentment that had threatened to tear them apart.

"Thanks, Vance (Eddie)," Eddie (Vance) whispered, his voice barely above a whisper. "I'm gonna miss her."

And as they stood together in the fading light of dusk, Eddie (Vance) knew that their grief had forged an unlikely bond between them – a bond born of loss and sorrow but tempered by the enduring power of love and forgiveness. At that moment, Eddie (Vance) found solace in the knowledge that Susan's legacy would live on in the hearts of those she had loved and touched – a beacon of hope and healing in the darkness of their grief.

Chapter 15

It had been a couple of years since Susan's death, and the pain, though dulled with time, was still a constant companion for Eddie (Vance). The days had turned into weeks, and the weeks into months, each one blending into the next with a monotony that Eddie (Vance)had come to accept as part of his new normal. Life had continued, as it always does, but there was an emptiness that lingered, a void that no amount of time seemed capable of filling.

Despite this, Eddie (Vance) had found a sense of purpose in his work at the hospital. It was here, amidst the sterile hallways and the hum of medical equipment, that he felt closest to Susan. She had always been passionate about helping others, and in a way, Eddie (Vance) felt he was honoring her memory by dedicating himself to his patients. It was in this familiar routine that he found a semblance of peace.

But life, as unpredictable as it is, had other plans for Eddie (Vance). It was on a particularly hectic day in the emergency room that he met her – a young woman named Emily, who had recently joined the hospital staff as a nurse. She was kind, attentive, and possessed a warmth that reminded Eddie (Vance) of Susan in many ways, though she was distinctly her own person.

Their first encounter was unremarkable on the surface. Emily had approached Eddie (Vance) with a question about a patient's chart; her brow furrowed in concentration. He had answered her query with his usual professionalism, but there was something in her eyes – a spark of curiosity and kindness – that caught his attention. Over the next few weeks, their paths crossed more frequently, and Eddie (Vance) found himself looking forward to their interactions.

It started with small conversations shared during brief moments of respite amidst the chaos of the hospital. Emily had a way of making even the most mundane topics seem interesting, and Eddie (Vance) was surprised at how easily he found himself opening up to her. She spoke about her love for hiking and her passion for painting, and Eddie (Vance) shared stories about his childhood and his life before Susan's illness.

One evening, after a particularly grueling shift, Eddie (Vance) and Emily found themselves alone in the break room. The hospital was unusually quiet, the kind of stillness that felt almost sacred. Emily was sipping a cup of tea, her eyes thoughtful as she gazed out the window. Eddie (Vance) took a seat across from her, feeling a sudden, inexplicable urge to share something he had kept buried for so long.

"You know, Susan would have liked you," he said quietly, breaking the silence.

Emily turned to him, her expression gentle and understanding. "You talk about her a lot," she observed. "She must have been very special."

"She was," Eddie (Vance) replied, his voice tinged with a mixture of sorrow and fondness. "She had this incredible way of making everyone around her feel important. Losing her... it was the hardest thing I've ever gone through."

Emily reached out, placing a comforting hand on his. "I can't imagine how difficult that must have been," she said softly. "But

I believe that people like Susan leave behind a legacy of love and kindness that continues to touch the lives of those they leave behind."

Eddie (Vance) felt a lump form in his throat, her words resonating deeply within him. For the first time in a long while, he felt a flicker of hope, a sense that maybe, just maybe, he could find happiness again. As he looked into Emily's eyes, he saw a future that was not overshadowed by the past but rather illuminated by the love and memories he carried with him.

Over the next few months, Eddie (Vance) and Emily grew closer. Their bond, initially forged through shared experiences at work, deepened into something more profound. Emily's presence brought a lightness to Eddie (Vance)'s life that he hadn't felt in years, and he found himself daring to dream of a future that included love once more.

One evening, as they sat on the rooftop of the hospital watching the sunset, Eddie (Vance) turned to Emily, his heart pounding in his chest. "Emily, I want you to know how much you mean to me," he began, his voice steady but filled with emotion. "You've brought so much joy into my life, and I thank you for being on this journey with me."

Emily smiled, her eyes shimmering with tears. "I feel the same way, Eddie (Vance). You've shown me what it means to truly care for someone, and I'm grateful every day for the chance to be a part of your life."

At that moment, Eddie (Vance) felt a sense of peace and fulfillment that he hadn't thought possible since Susan's passing. He knew that the road ahead would not be without its challenges, but with Emily by his side, he felt ready to face whatever came their way. Together, they would honor Susan's memory by embracing the love and happiness that life had to offer, knowing that the past had shaped them, but it did not define them.

***

The days had grown warmer, and the hospital was buzzing with the seasonal influx of patients. Eddie (Vance) found himself busier than ever, but amidst the whirlwind of work, his thoughts often drifted to Emily. Their budding relationship had become a bright spot in his life, and he felt a renewed sense of optimism and joy. However, as their bond deepened, Eddie (Vance) knew there was a significant step he needed to consider—introducing Emily to Megan, his daughter.

One evening, after a particularly long shift, Eddie (Vance) decided to seek out Vance (Eddie). They had maintained a tentative but respectful friendship since Susan's funeral, their shared grief forging an unspoken understanding between them. Vance (Eddie) knew both the light and the dark sides of his life, and Eddie (Vance) valued his perspective.

Eddie (Vance) found Vance (Eddie) in the hospital cafeteria, nursing a cup of coffee. The weariness in Vance (Eddie)'s eyes mirrored his own, but there was a warmth there that spoke of mutual respect.

"Hey, Vance (Eddie)," Eddie (Vance) greeted as he sat down across from him.

Vance (Eddie) looked up, a faint smile crossing his lips. "Hey, Eddie (Vance). How are things?"

Eddie (Vance) hesitated for a moment, then decided to plunge into the topic that had been on his mind. "Actually, I wanted to talk to you about something important. It's about Emily."

Vance (Eddie) raised an eyebrow, his interest piqued. "Emily? The new nurse you've been seeing?"

"Yeah, that's her," Eddie (Vance) confirmed, taking a deep breath. "Things are getting serious between us, and I'm thinking about introducing her to Megan. I just... I want to make sure it's the right time."

Vance (Eddie)'s expression grew thoughtful, and he took a sip of his coffee before responding. "Introducing someone new to your daughter is a big step, Eddie (Vance). It's good that you're thinking carefully about it. How much do you really know about Emily?"

Eddie (Vance)nodded, appreciating Vance (Eddie)'s candidness. "I know she's kind and compassionate and that she loves her job. We've spent a lot of time together to know that she's someone who could be a positive influence in Megan's life. But maybe you're right. Maybe I should learn more about her background before taking this step."

Vance (Eddie) leaned back in his chair, considering his words. "I'm not saying Emily isn't a great person. From what you've told me, she sounds wonderful. But Megan's been through a lot. Losing Mom was hard on all of us, but especially on her. You need to be absolutely sure that introducing Emily won't disrupt the progress Megan's made."

Eddie (Vance) sighed, running a hand through his hair. "I know, Vance (Eddie). I just want Megan to see that there's still happiness and love in the world. I want her to know that it's okay to move forward."

"And she will, in time," Vance (Eddie) said gently. "But remember, she looks up to you. She needs to see that you're making thoughtful decisions. Why don't you spend some more time with Emily outside of work? See how she is in different settings and how she handles various situations. Get to know her a bit more deeply."

Eddie (Vance) nodded, absorbing Vance (Eddie)'s advice. "You're right. I'll take it slow and make sure it's the right decision for both Megan and me."

As Eddie (Vance) left the cafeteria, he felt a renewed sense of purpose. He would take the time to learn more about Emily, understand the depths of her character, and ensure that she was truly someone who could bring joy and stability to Megan's life.

The next few weeks were filled with new experiences. Eddie (Vance) and Emily explored their city, visiting parks, attending local events, and even taking a short weekend trip to the coast. Eddie (Vance) watched closely how Emily interacted with strangers, how she handled unexpected challenges, and how she responded to the world around her. Each day, he found himself more impressed by her kindness, her patience, and her unwavering positivity.

One afternoon, as they sat on a bench overlooking the ocean, Eddie (Vance) decided it was time to share more about his life with Emily. He had mentioned Megan in passing, but now he wanted to delve deeper.

"Emily, there's something important I need to talk to you about," he began, his voice steady but serious.

Emily turned to him, her eyes full of concern. "Of course, Eddie (Vance). What's on your mind?"

He took a deep breath, gathering his thoughts. "I've really enjoyed our time together, and I feel like we're building something special. But there's a part of my life that I want you to know more about—my daughter, Megan."

Emily's expression softened, and she reached out to hold his hand. "I'd love to hear more about her, Eddie (Vance). I know she means the world to you."

Eddie (Vance) smiled, feeling a sense of relief. "She does. Megan is an amazing girl, but she's been through a lot. Losing her mother was incredibly hard on her, and I've been trying to help her navigate that loss. I want to make sure that introducing you to her is the right step and that it won't disrupt her healing process."

Emily nodded her grip on his hand, firm and reassuring. "I understand, Eddie (Vance). And I appreciate how thoughtful you're being about this. I want to be a positive influence in Megan's life, but I agree that we should take things one step at a time."

As they sat together, watching the waves crash against the shore, Eddie (Vance) felt a profound sense of gratitude. With Emily's understanding and support, he felt more confident about the future. He knew that by taking things slowly and being mindful of Megan's needs, they could build a new chapter filled with love, hope, and healing.

***

As Eddie (Vance)'s relationship with Emily continued to blossom, he couldn't shake the feeling of unease that had settled in the pit of his stomach. Despite her warmth and kindness, there were moments when he caught glimpses of a shadow lurking beneath her cheerful demeanor—a shadow that whispered secrets and hidden truths.

It was on a seemingly ordinary day in the hospital that Eddie (Vance)'s suspicions were confirmed. He had been called to the pharmacy to review inventory discrepancies, a routine task that he performed regularly as part of his administrative duties. As he meticulously combed through the records, his eyes narrowed in disbelief at what he discovered.

There, in black and white, was evidence of missing medication—pills and vials of controlled substances that had inexplicably vanished from the shelves. Eddie (Vance)'s heart sank as he realized the implications of what he was seeing. Someone within the hospital staff was stealing drugs, and the evidence pointed to one person in particular—Emily.

He couldn't bring himself to believe it at first. Emily, with her kind eyes and infectious laughter, couldn't possibly be involved in such nefarious activities. But the evidence was irrefutable, and Eddie (Vance) knew that he had a duty to report what he had found.

With a heavy heart, Eddie (Vance) approached his supervisor and presented his findings. The ensuing investigation was swift and thorough, culminating in Emily's dismissal from her position at the hospital. Eddie (Vance) watched in silence as she was escorted from the premises, her expression a mixture of shock and betrayal.

In the days that followed, Eddie (Vance) wrestled with conflicting emotions. He couldn't reconcile the image of the woman he had grown to care for with the reality of her actions. He had trusted Emily implicitly, had believed in the goodness of her heart, and yet she had betrayed that trust in the most egregious way possible.

When Emily confronted him about her termination, Eddie (Vance) struggled to find the right words. He explained what he had discovered, his voice heavy with regret and disappointment. Emily denied any wrongdoing at first, but as Eddie (Vance) presented the evidence against her, her facade crumbled.

"I can't believe you would think I'm capable of something like this," Emily cried, her voice breaking with emotion.

Vance felt a pang of guilt, but he knew that he had no choice but to stand by his principles. "I'm sorry, Emily. But the evidence speaks for itself. I trusted you, and you violated that trust in the worst way possible."

Their relationship ended that day, shattered by the weight of betrayal and deceit. Eddie (Vance) couldn't bring himself to look at Emily without seeing the shadow of doubt that now clouded his perception of her. He had believed in her goodness and had seen a future filled with love and happiness, but now all he felt was the bitter sting of betrayal.

In the days that followed, Eddie (Vance) immersed himself in his work, seeking solace in the familiar routine of the hospital. He couldn't erase the pain of what had happened, but he found comfort in the knowledge that he had done the right thing, even if it had come at a great personal cost.

As he watched Emily walk away from his life, Eddie (Vance) knew that he would never forget the lessons he had learned. Trust was a fragile thing, easily broken and difficult to repair. But he refused to let the actions of one person define his future. With each passing day, he would strive to rebuild the trust that had been shattered, knowing that true love and happiness were worth fighting for, no matter the obstacles that stood in his way.

Chapter 16

Vance (Eddie) had always been one to drift through life with a sense of detachment, a defense mechanism honed from years of loss and heartache. His mother's death had left a scar that no amount of time or distance could ever fully heal. Yet, amidst the bleakness of his past, there had always been a faint glimmer of hope that reignited the day he reconnected with Jennifer.

It was at a local charity event, a fundraiser for the hospital's new pediatric wing, that Vance (Eddie) noticed someone who looked like Jennifer.

Jennifer had been away from home for quite some time. Susan and John had not told her about her being adopted, and when she found it, it brought a spiral of emotions upon her. Being in her rebellious phase in high school, she left home one night and was determined never to return.

That evening, as Vance (Eddie) stood by the refreshments table, he caught sight of Jennifer across the room. She looked much the same — perhaps a bit older, but with the same warmth in her eyes and the same radiant smile. It took him a moment to gather the courage to approach her, his heart pounding with a mix of excitement and trepidation.

"Jennifer?" he called out, his voice wavering slightly.

She turned toward him, her eyes widening in recognition. "Vance! Is that really you?" she exclaimed, a genuine smile spreading across her face.

They embraced, the years melting away as they fell into an easy conversation. They spoke of old times, shared memories, and the winding paths their lives had taken. Jennifer had become a social worker, dedicating her life to helping children and families in need. Vance (Eddie) was nothing but proud to see his sister this successful and happy.

Their reconnection felt like a chance at something new, a possibility Eddie (Vance) had almost forgotten. Over the next few months, they spent more time together, rekindling the bond they once shared. They attended community events, helping those in need whenever they could find the opportunity.

It was on one such evening, as they sat in a cozy café, that Vance (Eddie) decided to open up about Susan's death. They talked about Susan and how, in her last days, when cancer had completely overpowered her body, she wished to see Jennifer again and tell her how her family was incomplete without her. As Vance (Eddie) told her this, Jennifer regretted not staying in touch with anyone.

"I'm so sorry I couldn't be there," she said, tears streaming down her face.

"I know mom hid a lot of things from you, but know that you'll always be family. I have always treated you like a sister, and I will continue to do so," Vance (Eddie) reassured her.

Jennifer nodded and smiled as she felt safe around Vance (Eddie). They grew closer with each passing day, their bond deepening as they moved back into Susan's old house. Living in that house made them rethink the memories that they had kept together as a family; it made them feel at home.

One day, Jennifer asked, “Is Eddie (Vance)… still around?”

“Do you want to meet him?” Vance (Eddie) inquired.

She nodded softly, which led to Vance (Eddie) arranging a dinner. He knew how Jennifer and Eddie (Vance) had ended their relationship back in high school when Jennifer cheated on him. But he understood that they were children back then, and a lot had happened since then. A simple and peaceful family dinner wouldn’t hurt anyone. This would also allow Jennifer to finally meet Megan, whom she had heard so much about from Vance (Eddie).

He spoke to Eddie (Vance) about Jennifer’s return, and even though he was skeptical at first, he ultimately agreed to meet her.

The evening of the dinner arrived. Jennifer felt nervous; she knew meeting him would not be easy. She wanted to put the past behind them and show Eddie (Vance) and Megan that she genuinely cared about them. But it was understandable that Eddie (Vance) would be extremely hard to comply with.

***

Eddie (Vance) entered the diner and greeted them. His smile seemed non-existent at first, but he welcomed Jennifer.

"It’s been a while,” he said.

Jennifer passed a smile, feeling a bit nervous. "It has… How have you been?”

“We are learning to survive.” He smiled, then pointed toward the little girl whose hand he was holding, “This is Megan.”

Megan, a bit shy at first, observed Jennifer with curious eyes. Jennifer knelt down to her level, her voice gentle and warm. "Hi, Megan. It's really nice to meet you."

Megan smiled tentatively, her initial shyness giving way to curiosity. "Hello. Do you like dogs? We have a dog named Max."

Jennifer's face lit up. "I love dogs! I can't wait to meet Max."

With the ice broken, the rest of the evening flowed smoothly. Vance (Eddie) shared stories and laughter over a meal; the atmosphere, though dim and cold, slowly emanated warmth. Jennifer and Megan bonded over their mutual love of animals, and by the end of the evening, Megan was chattering away excitedly about all the things she wanted to show Jennifer.

As they prepared to leave, Vance (Eddie) pulled Eddie (Vance) aside. "You both were kids; let it go now." But Eddie (Vance) offered no answer.

"You do know you have to get over all of this soon enough, I understand. Losing mom... It has been hard for you, but you have to get through it."

"I'll see through it," Eddie (Vance) replied. "I have Megan to take care of."

He began walking off, but Vance pulled on him, "If you want... I can ask Jennifer to accompany you. She's good with kids."

Eddie (Vance) looked at him and nodded as he put on his coat.

On their way to the car, Eddie (Vance) helped Megan in the car first. But as soon as he was about to enter, Jennifer interrupted him. "It's been ages since what happened; you're still not over it?"

"Now is not the best time to discuss this," Eddie (Vance) responded.

"Please, we were kids. I want to help. Vance has told me about you and.... Mom.... It must have been difficult for you," Jennifer added as she rested her palm on his shoulder.

"Don't try to sympathize. I am fine. I will give you a call if I need you," he added before sitting in the car and zooming off to his place whilst Jennifer was left standing. She felt the pain coursing through her veins; it was extremely terrible to watch him in this state.

Jennifer sighed and eventually made it back to her place with her brother. It was a difficult night, but she knew that Eddie (Vance) needed help. She had been through something similar.

Jennifer had separated from her husband after giving birth to Jacob. Her husband was a gambler and an alcoholic, and he would often beat her to make her listen to his egoistic approach toward life; he would gamble all of Jennifer's money and physically assault her if she ever decided to intervene. She became homeless after a few months and decided to make a change.

She got a new job as a social worker and dedicated her life to helping those in need who could not fend for themselves; it was a noble occupation, and she loved every second of it.

***

A few days later, Eddie (Vance) was left alone in his room, drinking. His heart ached from the pain that he faced during the events that had occurred in life, and he wanted ease. Earning for

Megan had become a hassle, too, since as the child grew, so did her needs. It was a harsh reality he was gripping all alone, and for a second, he did think about the offer Vance (Eddie) posed.

Without another thought, he called Jennifer over and asked her if she could stay at his place and take care of Megan. Jennifer agreed reluctantly, but that was not the only thing in Eddie (Vance)'s mind.

In a few hours, Jennifer eventually approached the door and entered the house. She looked at him with a questioning look since Megan was asleep, but at a moment's notice, Eddie (Vance)'s lips locked into hers.

Jennifer recognized that Eddie (Vance) was alone and suffering; the stench of alcohol was unbearable, but she went on with it. She, too, had pent up emotions that she needed to address, but right now, all she could think about was do this with Eddie (Vance).

Their lips danced aggressively, and as they approached Eddie (Vance)'s room, they were stripped of their clothes. Eddie (Vance) and Jennifer spent the entire night pleasing each other in the dimly lit room, having no restraints or boundaries nor caring for the repercussions of their deeds. It was a night of letting out their emotional turmoil in the form of intercourse.

***

From that moment, Eddie (Vance) and Jennifer rekindled their bond together. They would spend countless nights pleasing each other and not feel guilty about their actions. Eddie (Vance) knew deep down he wanted Jennifer ever since high school, but her actions had led them to their separation. He could tell now that

Jennifer wanted to fix what she had broken in between them, and it eventually bloomed into them being in love all over again.

Eddie (Vance) and Jennifer sat, discussing the events of the days they had spent together. "Megan really seems to take to you," Eddie (Vance) said, his voice warm with appreciation.

Jennifer smiled, her eyes lighting up. "She's a wonderful girl, Eddie. I loved spending time with her. It means a lot to me that she feels comfortable around me."

"I think she sees the kindness in you that I once saw," Eddie (Vance) replied. He hesitated for a moment before continuing, "I also want to talk about your son, Jacob. I want to understand more about your life and how he fits into it."

Jennifer's expression softened. "Jacob is my world. He's a bright, curious boy, and he's been my rock through everything. I want you to meet him, Eddie. It's important to me that you get to know each other."

Eddie (Vance) nodded, feeling a sense of connection deepen between them. "I'd like that, Jennifer. I want to be a part of your life, all of it. I know that building a future together means embracing our pasts and the people we care about."

As they sipped their coffee, Eddie (Vance) felt a renewed sense of hope. He and Jennifer were navigating their relationship with honesty and care, each step bringing them closer to the life they both longed for. With Megan and Jacob as part of their journey, Eddie (Vance) knew that their future, though uncertain, was filled with the promise of love and understanding.

***

A year into their new relationship, Eddie (Vance) and Jennifer had settled into a comfortable routine. Their bond grew stronger with each passing day, and they spent much of their time together with Megan and Jacob, forming a blended family that filled Eddie (Vance)'s heart with a joy he hadn't known in years.

One bright spring morning, Jennifer and Eddie (Vance) sat on their porch, sipping coffee and enjoying the gentle warmth of the sun. Jennifer had been feeling off for a few weeks, a subtle change she couldn't quite put her finger on. Today, she decided it was time to share her suspicions with Eddie (Vance).

"Eddie," she began, her voice hesitant but filled with excitement, "there's something I need to tell you."

Eddie (Vance) looked at her, his eyes filled with concern. "What is it, Jennifer? Is everything okay?"

Jennifer took a deep breath, her eyes shining. "I think I might be pregnant."

Eddie (Vance)'s heart skipped a beat, and he reached out to take her hand. "Really? Are you sure?"

"I took a test this morning," Jennifer said, her smile widening. "It was positive."

A wave of emotions washed over Eddie (Vance)—joy, excitement, and a touch of nervousness. He pulled Jennifer into a tight embrace, his heart racing. "This is incredible news, Jennifer. I can't believe it."

As the weeks passed, their excitement grew. Jennifer's pregnancy brought a new sense of purpose and anticipation to their lives. They shared the news with Vance, Megan, and Jacob, who were all thrilled about the upcoming addition to their family.

Nine months later, on a crisp autumn day, Jennifer gave birth to a healthy baby boy. They named him Jonathon Jr. Holding his newborn son for the first time, Eddie (Vance) felt a profound sense of love and gratitude. He looked at Jennifer, her face glowing with happiness, and knew that their journey together was only beginning.

The days that followed were filled with sleepless nights, joyful moments, and the challenges that come with raising a newborn. Eddie (Vance) and Jennifer navigated these challenges together, their bond stronger than ever. Megan and Jacob adored their baby brother, often vying for the chance to hold him and make him smile.

One evening, as Eddie (Vance) rocked Jonathon Jr. to sleep, he reflected on the path that had brought them to this moment. The pain of the past, the struggles, and the healing had all led to this—the creation of a new family filled with love and hope.

As Jonathon Jr. drifted off to sleep in his arms, Eddie (Vance) felt a deep sense of peace. With Jennifer by his side and their children surrounding them with laughter and love, he knew that they were ready to face whatever the future held. Together, they would embrace each new day, their hearts united by the love they had found and the family they had built.

The following weekend, the entire family gathered at the park to celebrate Jonathon Jr.'s arrival. Eddie (Vance) manned the grill while Megan and Jacob played tag, their laughter filling the air.

Jennifer sat on a picnic blanket, cradling Jonathon Jr., her eyes soft with contentment.

Eddie (Vance) joined her, wrapping an arm around her shoulders. "Look at us," he said, his voice filled with awe. "We've come so far."

Jennifer leaned into him, her smile radiant. "We have. And it's only going to get better."

As they watched Megan and Jacob run around and felt the warmth of Jonathon Jr. in their arms, Eddie (Vance) knew that he had found his forever family. The future was bright, and he was ready to embrace it with Jennifer and their children by his side. Together, they would face any challenges that came their way, confident in the strength of their love and the bond that held them together.

Chapter 17

It had been a few years since Jennifer and Eddie (Vance) had been dating. Being of the same age, Megan and Jacob had quickly grown accustomed to each other's company and enjoyed their playtime together.

As Eddie (Vance) hit the mark of forty, his health began to deteriorate. What he perceived as a simple decline in health due to aging, the constant queasiness in his stomach, followed by vomiting and pained blood coughs, pushed him to consult a doctor.

The warm glow of the morning sun filtered through the curtains as Eddie (Vance) sat in his doctor's office, his mind reeling from the news he had just received; a spiral of diagnosis after a number of hospital visits identified that Eddie (Vance) was experiencing chronic kidney failure, exacerbated due to his excessive usage of alcohol.

The words "kidney failure" and "dialysis" echoed in his ears, each syllable heavy with uncertainty and fear. Dr. Patterson, his physician, had explained the situation with calm professionalism, but the gravity of the situation was undeniable.

"Your kidney has suffered from the formation of critical ulcers and stones that are now embedded deep into it. We need to start looking for a donor immediately," Dr. Patterson said gently, his eyes filled with concern. "Time is of the essence, Eddie."

Eddie (Vance) nodded, his throat tight with emotion. "I understand. I'll talk to my family about it."

Jennifer discussed with Eddie (Vance) that they should start the dialysis process as soon as possible. Eddie (Vance) agreed and thus began the biweekly visits to the dialysis center while they continued to look for a doner for him.

***

In the evening, Eddie (Vance) sat with Jennifer on their porch, the weight of the conversation heavy between them. Jennifer listened intently as Eddie (Vance) explained his diagnosis and the need for a transplant. Her eyes filled with determination and love as she took his hand in hers.

"We'll get through this, Eddie. We'll find a donor," she said firmly.

"I know," Eddie (Vance) replied, his voice tinged with worry. "But it's not that simple. Finding a match can take time, and I don't know how long I have before my kidneys give up on me."

Jennifer's grip on his hand tightened. "We'll start with the family. I'll get tested first. We're in this together."

The following week, Jennifer went through the necessary tests to determine if she could be a donor. The wait for the results was excruciating, each passing day filled with anxiety and hope. Finally, the call came, and Jennifer's face lit up with relief as she heard the news.

"Eddie, I'm a match!" she announced, her voice trembling with emotion. "I can be your donor."

Tears welled up in Eddie (Vance)'s eyes as he pulled her into a tight embrace. "Thank you, Jennifer. I don't know how to even begin to express my gratitude."

"This is what family is for, Eddie; you don't have to thank me, " Jennifer whispered, her voice breaking.

The weeks leading up to the transplant were a whirlwind of preparations and medical appointments. Jennifer's determination never wavered, and Eddie (Vance) drew strength from her unwavering support. Their family rallied around them, offering words of encouragement and love.

The day of the surgery arrived, and Eddie (Vance) and Jennifer found themselves side by side in the hospital, their hands intertwined. As they were wheeled into the operating rooms, they exchanged a final look of reassurance and love.

***

Hours later, the surgery was declared a success. Eddie (Vance) awoke to find Jennifer in the bed next to his, her smile weary but triumphant. "We did it," she said softly, her eyes filled with tears of relief.

Eddie (Vance) squeezed her hand, his heart overflowing with gratitude. "You saved my life, Jennifer. I can't thank you enough."

In the weeks that followed, Eddie (Vance)'s health improved steadily. Jennifer, despite her own recovery, remained a constant source of strength and support. Their bond grew even stronger, forged in the fire of adversity.

One afternoon, as they sat on their porch watching Megan and Jacob play with Jonathon Jr., Eddie (Vance) turned to Jennifer, his eyes reflecting the depth of his love and appreciation.

"You've given me so much, Jennifer. A second chance at life, our beautiful family, and a future filled with hope. I don't know how I got so lucky."

Jennifer smiled, her eyes shining with emotion. "We're lucky to have each other, Eddie. And together, there's nothing we can't overcome."

As the sun set on the horizon, casting a golden glow over their home, Eddie (Vance) felt a profound sense of peace. With Jennifer by his side and their family's unwavering support, he knew that they were ready to face whatever challenges lay ahead. Their love, tested and proven, would see them through any storm, illuminating their path with hope and strength.

Eddie (Vance) looked out at the setting sun, its golden rays casting a warm glow over the horizon. The evening breeze whispered through the trees, carrying with it the promise of a new day. As he sat with Jennifer on their porch, surrounded by the sounds of laughter and the gentle hum of life, Eddie (Vance) felt a sense of peace wash over him.

"Jennifer," he began, his voice soft but resolute, "there's something I need to tell you."

Jennifer turned to him, her eyes filled with concern. "What is it, Eddie?"

"I made a promise to Susan," Eddie (Vance) said, his voice tinged with emotion. "A promise to honor her memory and to keep her love alive in our hearts."

Jennifer reached out to take his hand, her touch comforting and warm. "I understand, Eddie. Mom was a big part of your life, and her memory will always be a part of ours."

Eddie (Vance) nodded, a faint smile playing at the corners of his lips. "But it's more than just a memory, Jennifer. It's a vow to live each day with purpose, to cherish the moments we have together, and to never take our love for granted."

Jennifer squeezed his hand, her eyes filled with understanding. "I'll always be here for you, Eddie. Through thick and thin, in good times and bad."

As they sat together in the fading light, Eddie (Vance) felt a renewed sense of determination wash over him. He knew that he could keep his promise to Susan—to live each day with gratitude and to embrace the beauty of life, even in the face of adversity.

As the stars began to twinkle in the night sky, Eddie (Vance) and Jennifer sat in comfortable silence, their hearts united by a love that transcended time and space. Together, they would navigate the journey ahead, their bond stronger than ever, and their spirits filled with hope. And as they watched their children play in the fading light, Eddie (Vance) knew that Susan's love would always be with them, guiding them on their path and lighting the way forward.

***

Even though he had felt relieved from the pain that lingered in his body, another memory refused to be silenced – the raw pain etched on Susan's face as she confessed the assault she had endured at thirteen. It was a searing brand on his soul, a lit match igniting a fire of righteous fury within him. He wouldn't let her trauma be buried with her. Justice, for Susan, became his obsession.

He looked through different records and documents from Susan's house to search for clues. All these clues led him to the hospital he was born in. However, he kept it hidden from Jennifer since he did not want her to know all the things Susan had told her; he knew it would destroy her.

The hospital library, a forgotten corner usually echoing with the hushed whispers of turning pages, became Eddie (Vance)'s sanctuary. Here, amidst the worn spines and musty scent of knowledge, he could escape the confines of his room. He devoured books on forensic science with the hunger of a man lost in the desert. Every page held the potential to be a weapon, every research paper a map leading him out of the labyrinth of grief and toward the truth.

One night, Eddie (Vance) stumbled upon an article titled "Cracking Cold Cases: The Rise of Forensic Technology." The title was a siren song, luring him deeper into the world of advancements that could potentially breathe new life into forgotten investigations. He read about DNA analysis, a revolutionary tool with the power to identify perpetrators from decades-old evidence. Fingerprint identification, once limited by technology, now boasted incredible precision. Digital forensics, a relatively new frontier, promised to unlock secrets hidden within the digital footprints left behind. Hope, a fragile ember, flickered to life within him. These advancements were not just tools; they were lighthouses in the storm, guiding him toward the possibility of exposing Susan's assailant.

The vow he silently made to Susan became a mantra that fueled his research. He wasn't just reading; he was strategizing. He contacted forensic experts, their voices a comforting hum on the phone, offering guidance and expertise. Each conversation was a piece of the puzzle falling into place, a confirmation that he was on the right path. This wasn't just about bringing her attacker to justice; it was about honoring Susan, about ensuring that the trauma she endured wouldn't be silenced.

Each new discovery in the realm of forensic science wasn't just another piece of information for Eddie (Vance); it was a brick laid on the path to healing. The gnawing emptiness that had taken root within him began to recede, replaced by a quiet, steady determination. Susan's memory, once a source of raw pain, transformed into a guiding light. Her courage, the very quality that allowed her to share her trauma, became a beacon that pushed Eddie (Vance) forward in his relentless pursuit of justice.

With every intricate detail, he absorbed – the power of a single hair follicle for DNA analysis, the uniqueness of a fingerprint, the ability to extract digital evidence from forgotten devices – Eddie (Vance) felt a growing sense of empowerment. Each fact wasn't just theoretical knowledge; it was a potential weapon in his arsenal, a tool that brought him closer to fulfilling the promise he'd silently made to Susan.

This promise transcended simply seeking justice for her. It became a vow to himself, a way to honor Susan's spirit. He wouldn't let her story be buried alongside her. He would ensure that the trauma she endured wouldn't become another silenced scream in the dark.

The sterile white walls of the hospital room, once a constant reminder of his loss, slowly began to fade away. In their place, a new vision emerged. He saw a future where Susan's story wouldn't be another unsolved mystery gathering dust in a forgotten file. Instead, it would become a testament to the enduring power of truth and the unwavering pursuit of justice.

It would be a beacon of hope for others who had suffered in silence, a symbol that even in the face of immense loss and delayed accountability, the fight for justice could still prevail. Eddie (Vance) knew the road ahead wouldn't be easy. There would be setbacks, frustrations, and moments of doubt. But with Susan's memory as his guiding light and the power of forensic science as his weapon, he was determined to see his promise through. He would bring her assailant to justice and, in doing so, ensure that Susan's story became a testament to the enduring human spirit.

Chapter 18

Discharged from the confines of the hospital, Eddie (Vance) made a run for it as he carried with him all the evidence of the forensics that could lead to all the information that he needed to help Susan's case. The world outside, once muted by grief, now exploded with symphonies of life. Eddie (Vance) was determined to cherish Susan's vow, but what he was about to find out would leave a stain on himself for the rest of his life.

Amidst the newfound determination, a nagging curiosity lingered. The revelation of Jennifer's perfect match as a donor had sparked a question that had festered within him for quite some time. He was questioning the true nature of his heritage.

Moreover, Eddie (Vance) had always felt a sense of disconnect from his family, a hollowness that could not be filled with the explanations that were provided to him as a child. He took a DNA test to be sure. The swab felt insignificant in his hand, a tiny instrument holding the potential to rewrite his understanding of himself.

Weeks later, the email arrived. Its sterile subject line – "Ancestry Results," paved the way for the emotional turmoil within Eddie (Vance). He clicked on the link and scrolled through the percentages detailing his genetic makeup as his heart was pounding against his ribs frantically. He quickly detected an anomaly.

"This can't be true..." He noticed the familiar ancestry in his results, "East Asian – 22%," it read.

Confusion morphed into a cold dread that settled in his gut. The memory of Susan's tearful confession on that fateful night surfaced – the sexual assault she had endured at a young age was not just tied to him but also had a horrific possibility that clawed its way to the forefront of his mind.

"Could it be...?"

He reread the email, innocuous percentages now holding a terrifying weight. He called the testing company, tremors tinging his voice as he requested to speak to a genetic counselor. The conversation that followed was a blur of technical terms and hushed explanations.

"Can you please speak in English?" Eddie (Vance) demanded desperately. The truth, delivered in a kind but firm voice, shattered the last vestiges of his reality.

Susan was not just the woman that he had fallen in love with; she was also his biological mother.

The revelation struck him like a physical blow. The woman he had cherished, the one whose memory fueled his crusade for justice, was not just a victim. She was the reason he existed. Grief, once a dull ache, roared back with renewed intensity, a suffocating wave that threatened to consume him entirely.

Questions began spiraling through his mind; he thought of the events that had occurred between him and her, all those countless nights of sleeping in the same bed, their daughter, and everything that happened between them. The horrors that followed clouded his mind.

The phone slipped from his hand, and he began vomiting. His mind was consumed by the thoughts of not just Susan but her mother, Hattie, and the death of Earl. Then came the thoughts of Jennifer, who he had dated as a child and had sex with quite recently. This made him think about Jonathan Jr. The idea of having a child with his half-sister made him hurl more violently. It was a disturbing night for him.

Disbelief hung heavy in the air, a shroud that choked off the oxygen of his previous understanding. How could years of yearning for a connection, the bottomless ache he'd attributed solely to adoption, have such a horrifying explanation all along? Susan, the woman he loved with a fierceness that rivaled the storm brewing inside him, had carried a secret so heavy it bent the very fabric of their reality.

The weight of this revelation threatened to shatter Eddie (Vance). It was a monstrous truth, exposing a darkness he wasn't sure he possessed. Yet, from the wreckage of his initial shock, a spark of defiance ignited. Susan's story wouldn't be buried by this monstrous secret. It wouldn't be another weight on her already burdened shoulders. No, it would be a testament, a blazing beacon to her strength. It would speak volumes of her courage, the depths of her will to survive, to raise a child, even when the very ground beneath her had crumbled. This wouldn't define her; it would be a mere chapter in the epic tale of her resilience. He wouldn't let it be anything less.

Eddie (Vance) spent the night in a waking nightmare. The revelation that Susan was his biological mother cast a long, grotesque shadow over everything he thought he knew about himself, his life, and his relationships. The love he shared with

Susan, the comfort he found in her arms, was now tainted by a horrifying truth. Disgust gnawed at him, twisting his insides into a knot.

Days bled into each other, a blur of nausea, emotional turmoil, and a desperate need for answers. He clung to the one shred of hope that remained – finding justice for Susan, his mother.

With trembling hands, he reached out to Vance (Eddie). The initial awkwardness of the conversation quickly dissipated as Eddie (Vance) poured out his story. Vance (Eddie) listened, his face a mask of disbelief that slowly morphed into understanding. He, too, had always felt a disconnect from his family, a yearning for something more.

Together, they delved back into the records of the hospital where they were born. The investigation, fueled by righteous anger, unearthed a startling truth. A single, overworked, and demonstrably underqualified nurse had been responsible for a series of mix-ups during a particularly busy shift. Eddie (Vance) and Vance (Eddie) were not the only ones switched at birth. There were others, their lives forever altered by a single moment of human error.

The revelation brought a twisted sense of relief. The blame, the sickening feeling of having violated Susan in some way, shifted. It wasn't his fault. It wasn't Vance (Eddie)'s fault. It was a cruel twist of fate, a bureaucratic nightmare that had shattered lives.

But anger simmered beneath the relief. How could such a crucial mistake have been allowed to happen? How many lives had been irrevocably altered by negligence? Eddie (Vance) was determined to hold the hospital accountable, to expose the cracks in the system that had caused so much pain.

He contacted a lawyer, a fierce woman with a steely gaze and a reputation for taking on seemingly impossible cases. The lawsuit, a David versus Goliath battle, became a new focus, a way to channel his grief and anger into something productive.

Yet, amidst the legal battles and the search for justice, Eddie (Vance) couldn't ignore the elephant in the room. What about Jennifer and Jonathan Jr.? The thought of them filled him with a dread that rivaled the initial shock of his discovery. He knew he had to address the situation, but the words seemed to stick in his throat, a bitter pill he couldn't swallow.

The lawsuit against the hospital became an all-consuming quest. News of the mix-up, a consequence of a single nurse's negligence, spread like wildfire. Eddie (Vance) found himself thrust into the spotlight, the face of a story that resonated with countless families forever altered by similar mistakes.

While the legal battle raged on, Eddie (Vance) couldn't shake the nagging feeling that something was missing. The answer to Susan's assault, the core reason for her emotional turmoil, remained shrouded in secrecy. The nurse responsible for the switch, a crucial piece of the puzzle, had vanished from official records. Determined to find her, Eddie (Vance) embarked on a relentless search, combing through dusty hospital archives and dead-end leads.

Weeks turned into months, frustration mounting with each dead end. Then, a breakthrough. A retired nurse, with a memory jogged by a news report, offered a glimmer of hope. She remembered the woman, a young, overwhelmed nurse struggling to keep afloat during a particularly demanding period.

Following this lead, Eddie (Vance) finally tracked her down, living a quiet life in a small rural town. The woman, weathered and weary, answered the door with a mix of surprise and trepidation. Inside, her story unfolded in a torrent of mumbled apologies and nervous glances. The hospital, she revealed, had fired her years ago, citing a string of errors, including the one that had switched Vance and Eddie.

Shame hung heavy in the air as Eddie (Vance) listened. The anger he'd harbored, the burning desire to hold someone accountable, began to ebb away. This woman, a victim of circumstance as much as he and Susan carried the weight of her mistakes for years.

"Did you ever know what happened to the babies you switched?" Eddie (Vance) asked, his voice devoid of accusation.

The woman shook her head, tears welling up in her eyes. "No. They let me go before they figured it all out. I... I'm so sorry."

Eddie (Vance) stood there, the weight of the past pressing down on him. The truth, while undeniably painful, offered a sliver of understanding. The assault Susan endured wasn't a consequence of their twisted family dynamic but a separate, horrifying event that had forever scarred her life.

Chapter 19

The sterile hum of the hospital monitors became a white noise lullaby, a constant reminder of the battle Susan had fought and ultimately lost. As Eddie (Vance) traced the outline of her empty bed with his gaze, a familiar ache settled in his chest. Her final moments replayed in his mind's eye - the struggle for breath, the weak squeeze of his hand, and the whispered promise that hung heavy in the air.

"Justice..." she had rasped, her voice barely audible. It was a simple word, yet it resonated with the weight of a thousand unspoken pleas. In that quiet hospital room, Eddie (Vance) had vowed to make good on that promise, to become the voice for the one she could no longer be.

Fueled by his vow, a new resolve hardened within him. He wouldn't let Susan's story become another statistic, another forgotten case file gathering dust on a shelf. The evidence, the very essence of her trauma, had to be somewhere. Armed with the newfound knowledge gleaned from countless hours in the hospital library, Eddie (Vance) knew his first step lay with the police department. The rape kit, a painful reminder of her ordeal, could potentially hold the key to identifying her attacker.

The prospect of revisiting the place where Susan's pain had been documented sent a tremor of apprehension through him. But the image of Susan's fragile hand intertwined with his fueled determination. Leaving the sterile haven of the hospital, he stepped back into the world, a warrior clad not in armor but in the righteousness of his cause. The police station loomed ahead, a fortress of bureaucracy, but Eddie (Vance) wouldn't be deterred. He had a promise to keep, and the pursuit of justice, however daunting, had officially begun.

The air in the police station hung heavy with a mix of stale coffee and nervous anticipation. Eddie (Vance) navigated the maze of desks, the fluorescent lights casting a sterile glow on the utilitarian space. He finally found the detective's office marked "Cold Case Unit" and took a deep breath before knocking.

A woman with eyes that had seen too much and a tired smile etched on her face answered the door. "Detective Miller?" Eddie (Vance) inquired, his voice surprisingly steady.

"Yes, how can I help you?" she replied, her gaze sharpening as she assessed the raw emotion etched on his face.

Eddie (Vance) explained his connection to Susan, the details of her case, and the promise he made on her deathbed. Detective Miller listened patiently, the weight of countless similar stories settling on her shoulders.

"Mr. Eddie (Vance)," she began, her voice gentle but firm, "I understand your pain and desire for justice. But cold cases are often years, even decades old. Evidence degrades, witnesses disappear, and leads run dry."

Eddie (Vance) wasn't deterred. He launched into a passionate explanation of his recent research, highlighting the advancements in forensic technology. "DNA analysis, fingerprint identification - wouldn't these techniques give you a fresh perspective on the evidence?"

Detective Miller's eyes flickered with interest. "Perhaps," she conceded, "but reopening a case takes time and resources. We have to prioritize based on potential leads and solvability."

Eddie (Vance) wasn't ready to back down. He presented the research papers he'd meticulously organized, highlighting specific techniques applicable to Susan's case. He spoke of the possibility of extracting digital evidence from her phone, a detail he hadn't even considered until his research delved into the power of digital forensics.

The detective studied the papers, a flicker of hope igniting in her gaze. Here was someone who hadn't given up, someone armed with knowledge and a burning desire for justice. "Look," she finally said, "I can't promise anything, but I'm willing to review the case file and see if there's anything new technology can reveal. However, it won't be a quick process."

Eddie (Vance)'s heart pounded with cautious optimism. "I understand," he replied, his voice thick with emotion, "but any progress, any chance to bring her attacker to justice, would be a step in the right direction."

Detective Miller nodded, a ghost of a smile playing on her lips. "Then let's take that step together, Mr. Eddie (Vance). We owe it to Susan and to everyone who deserves a voice."

Walking out of the station, Eddie (Vance) felt a weight lift from his shoulders. He hadn't achieved justice yet, but a seed of hope had been planted. He had found an ally, a champion for Susan's case. He knew the road ahead would be long, filled with bureaucratic hurdles and potential disappointments. But for the first time since Susan's passing, Eddie (Vance) felt a sense of purpose, a flicker of hope that her story wouldn't be another unsolved mystery lost in the labyrinth of time. He vowed to be there every step of the way, armed with his knowledge, his unwavering resolve, and the unrelenting memory of Susan's courage.

Days turned into weeks, then months, filled with a tense silence. Eddie (Vance) called Detective Miller regularly, his voice a mixture of hope and trepidation with each unanswered ring. Finally, one day, the call came.

"Mr. Eddie (Vance), it's Detective Miller," her voice sounded grave yet strangely hopeful. "We have a match."

Eddie (Vance)'s breath hitched in his throat. "A match? What do you mean?"

"The DNA analysis on the rape kit samples... it's a match to someone in the national database."

The world seemed to tilt on its axis. "Who is it?" Eddie (Vance)'s voice was a choked whisper.

A long pause followed, filled with the crackle of the phone line. Then, Detective Miller spoke, her voice barely a murmur, "Brian Breedlove."

The name hit Eddie (Vance) like an electric shock. Brian Breedlove - The man he'd called father all his life. The man who'd always seemed distant and cold, his touch a source of unease rather than comfort. The sickening realization crashed over him – the monster who'd shattered Susan's life was the very man he'd been raised to believe in.

A wave of nausea washed over him, threatening to pull him under. Grief, betrayal, and a white-hot rage churned within him. Susan's trusting eyes flashed in his mind, with her whispered plea for justice echoing in his ears. This wasn't just a revelation; it was an earthquake that had leveled the foundation of his reality.

"Mr. Eddie (Vance)? Are you there?" Detective Miller's voice cut through the fog of his emotions.

He took a shaky breath, forcing himself to speak. "Yes, Detective. I'm here."

"This must be a lot to process," she said, her voice filled with empathy. "We can discuss the next steps whenever you're ready."

Eddie (Vance) needed time. Time to absorb the horrifying truth, to grapple with the monstrous reality of his father. Time to turn the raw anger into a steely resolve, a determination to see Susan's attacker brought to justice, no matter the personal cost.

"Thank you, Detective," he croaked, his voice raw with emotion. "I'll... I'll need some time."

He hung up the phone, the weight of the revelation crushing him. The sterile white walls of his apartment seemed to mock him, a stark contrast to the turmoil raging within. He sank onto the couch, the familiar space suddenly tainted by the knowledge of the darkness it had harbored for years.

Days blurred into one another as Eddie (Vance) wrestled with his emotions. He found solace in Susan's memory, clutching the worn photograph of her radiant smile. It fueled his resolve, reminding him of the promise he made. He wouldn't let Brian

Breedlove get away with it. He would ensure Susan finally received the justice she deserved.

With renewed determination, Eddie (Vance) contacted Detective Miller. His voice, though laced with pain, was firm. "Let's bring him down," he said. "Let's make him pay for what he did."

The fight for justice had just begun, and this time, it was personal. Eddie (Vance) knew the road ahead wouldn't be easy. He would face not only the legal system but also the emotional turmoil of confronting the man who'd betrayed him in the most profound way. But he was no longer just a grieving man; he was Susan's advocate, armed with the truth and an unwavering will to see her story brought to light.

As Eddie (Vance) delved deeper into the investigation with Detective Miller, a horrifying truth began to unfold. The DNA match from Susan's rape kit wasn't an isolated incident. Further analysis revealed a disturbing pattern. Brian Breedlove's genetic profile linked him to a string of unsolved sexual assaults that had plagued the city for years. The realization sent a fresh wave of nausea churning through Eddie (Vance)'s gut. His father wasn't just a monster; he was a serial predator.

Detective Miller, her face grim, laid out the details. "These cases go back almost two decades, Mr. Eddie (Vance). Women from different walks of life, with no apparent connection. Cold cases that haunted us for years. Now, thanks to advancements in DNA technology and your persistence, we might finally bring closure to these victims and their families."

Eddie (Vance) felt a surge of conflicting emotions. Relief that Susan's attacker wouldn't get away with his crimes, but also a sickening sense of betrayal at the depth of his father's depravity. The man he'd known, the man who'd sat at the dinner table, who'd doled out punishments and dispensed (limited) affection, was a facade hiding a monstrous secret life.

As the investigation progressed, more victims came forward, their stories echoing Susan's with chilling similarity. Each account chipped away at the remaining fragments of the idealized father Eddie (Vance) had clung to. He learned of Brian's calculated methods, his predatory targeting, and the chilling manipulation he used to silence his victims.

The media picked up the story, painting a horrifying picture of Brian Breedlove, the seemingly respectable businessman who harbored a dark secret. Eddie (Vance) found himself thrust into the spotlight, a reluctant hero seeking justice for Susan and the countless other victims. He shared his story with the press, his voice cracking with emotion as he spoke of Susan's strength and the importance of breaking the silence surrounding sexual assault.

The public outcry was swift and fierce. Women who had suffered in silence found their voices, drawing strength from Susan's story and Eddie (Vance)'s unwavering pursuit of justice. The pressure mounted on the District Attorney's office, and Brian Breedlove's carefully constructed life began to crumble around him.

Facing a mountain of evidence and the weight of public opinion, Brian finally broke. He confessed to his crimes in a plea bargain, hoping to avoid the full force of the legal system. Eddie (Vance), though offered the chance to witness the confession, opted out. Hearing the details from his father's mouth felt like an unnecessary desecration of Susan's memory.

The trial was a swift and public affair. Brian Breedlove received a life sentence, a meager recompense for the devastation he had caused. As the gavel slammed down, Eddie (Vance) felt a bittersweet sense of closure. Susan and the other victims would never get their lives back, but at least their attacker was finally brought to justice.

Eddie (Vance)'s journey, however, had just begun. He dedicated himself to becoming an advocate for sexual assault victims, using his experience to raise awareness and fight for stronger legislation. Susan's memory became a beacon of hope, a testament to the enduring power of courage and the unwavering pursuit of justice. He knew the fight wouldn't be easy, but with each life he touched and each voice he empowered, he felt a flicker of peace. He was honoring Susan's memory, ensuring her story wouldn't be forgotten, and making a difference in the lives of others – a legacy far greater than the darkness that had preceded it.

The courtroom pulsed with a tense energy. Eddie (Vance) sat stiffly in the gallery, his gaze fixed on the hunched figure of Brian Breedlove. The man who had haunted his childhood and shattered Susan's life now appeared frail and diminished, a stark contrast to the imposing figure from Eddie (Vance)'s past. As the judge read the verdict, a life sentence without the possibility of parole, a wave of conflicting emotions washed over Eddie (Vance).

Relief flooded his system – Susan and the countless other victims had finally received a semblance of justice. Yet, a part of him couldn't shake the feeling of a hollow victory. Brian Breedlove, ravaged by age and likely facing a short time left, would spend his remaining years behind bars, a hollow shell of the predator he once was. The life sentence, while severe, felt almost merciful in the face of the devastation he'd caused.

Leaving the courthouse, Eddie (Vance) was met by a throng of reporters. Cameras flashed; microphones thrust in his face. But Eddie (Vance) had no grand pronouncements to make. He simply offered a quiet "Thank you" to the assembled crowd, acknowledging the support they had shown him and the other victims throughout the ordeal. He knew the media frenzy wouldn't last. But the impact of his actions, the fight for justice he had spearheaded, would hopefully leave a lasting mark.

In the following weeks, Eddie (Vance) poured himself into advocacy work. He connected with support groups for survivors of sexual assault, sharing his story and offering solace to those still grappling with the aftermath of their trauma. He lobbied for stricter legislation, pushing for reforms that would empower victims and hold perpetrators fully accountable. Susan's face, etched with a heartbreaking vulnerability, became a constant reminder of his purpose.

Life, however, rarely followed a neat narrative arc. One evening, a call came from Detective Miller. Brian Breedlove's health had deteriorated, and he was requesting a meeting with Eddie (Vance). A flicker of morbid curiosity sparked within him, a desire to confront the man who had irrevocably altered his life.

The prison visiting room was sterile and devoid of warmth. Brian, a skeletal shadow of his former self, looked up from the chair as Eddie (Vance) entered. The air crackled with a tension that transcended words.

"Eddie (Vance)," Brian rasped, his voice weak and halting. "I... I wanted to apologize."

Eddie (Vance) stared at him, a million emotions warring within him. Forgiveness felt like a betrayal of Susan and the other victims. Yet, the raw vulnerability in Brian's voice held a strange power.

"An apology," Eddie (Vance) finally spoke, his voice hoarse, "doesn't erase the damage you've caused. The lives you've shattered."

Brian nodded, tears welling up in his eyes. "I know. I know. There's no excuse for what I did. But... I hope you can find some peace, some closure."

Eddie (Vance) looked away, the image of Susan flashing in his mind. "Peace isn't something you can give me," he said finally. "But closure... maybe. Maybe that's something I can build."

He rose to leave, the weight of the encounter heavy on his shoulders. Brian's apology felt like a last-ditch attempt at redemption, a hollow offering that arrived too late. But as Eddie (Vance) walked out of the prison, he carried within him a newfound serenity. The fight for justice had taken its toll, but it had also empowered him.

***

Following the days of his encounter with him, Eddie (Vance) now sat across a room playing with Megan when Vance (Eddie) slowly approached the door to their house. Eddie (Vance) called him because he knew it was time to disclose the truth to someone who had always had his back, regardless of the severity of the situation.

"May I?" Vance (Eddie) smiled and offered Megan a cookie, which she cheerfully munched on.

"Thank you for coming at short notice," Eddie (Vance) mumbled as he watched him approach and sit next to him. "I... I met Brian Breedlove," he added.

"Who's that?" Vance (Eddie) inquired as he gave him a questioning look.

"The reason why we're all stuck in this mess..." Eddie (Vance) replied as his palms reached his forehead, pressing onto it.

"What's going on?" Vance (Eddie) leaned forward, resting his palm against his shoulder.

"I've lived your life, Vance (Eddie). And you've lived mine," Eddie (Vance) replied.

"I don't follow," Vance (Eddie) immediately retorted.

"We were both swapped at birth," Eddie (Vance) blurted, his eyes widened. His arms began shaking, and his eyes were now twitching.

"Eddie..." Vance (Eddie) was astonished and lost for words.

"Susan was raped; she conceived me in her womb. My father, or the man I referred to as my father all my life, Brian Breedlove, was responsible for it..." Eddie (Vance) looked at him with tears walloping in his eyes.

Vance (Eddie) stared at him blankly, trying to comprehend all that Eddie (Vance) was telling him.

"Your father is the reason all of this happened. And we are the ones that are paying the price for it," Eddie (Vance) added as he began to chuckle. His hysteria got the best of him, and his chuckles began to burst into an array of angst laughter.

"Calm down, Eddie..." Vance (Eddie) mumbled as he offered him a hug, but Eddie refused.

"This is so fucked up... Everything is so fucked up..." Eddie (Vance) shivered as he spoke. "What have I done...? Jennifer too...?"

"Eddie," Vance (Eddie) pulled him in a hug. "Calm down, I'm here, bud."

"What have I done, Vance (Eddie)..." Eddie (Vance) shuddered in his arms. "What have I done?"

"Everything will be alright; I promise..." Vance (Eddie) kept him safely in his arms as he allowed him to be vulnerable. They stayed in each other's arms for as long as Eddies (Vance) needed to, and later on, they decided to brew themselves a mug of coffee.

"Look, regardless of what happened, I think it was for the best. If Brian Breedlove is the man responsible for the birth of us both, that would mean we're both closer to each other than we truly believe," Vance (Eddie) spoke as he sipped.

"That would explain how it seemed easier for me to talk to you all the time," Eddie (Vance) replied as he nodded softly.

"Don't worry about Jennifer. You're both perfect for each other," Vance (Eddie) added, but it made Eddie (Vance) uncomfortable.

"Mom adopted her; she isn't related to us by blood," he added.

"That does not make it any better," Eddie (Vance) added as he scoffed and sipped.

"Look, whatever you do, don't compromise your health for it," Vance (Eddie) replied. "You know you need her," he added.

"He has been convicted for his crimes, Brian." Eddie (Vance) whispered.

"Susan was one hell of a good person. I hope you know that," he looked at Vance (Eddie) as he spoke, which made him nod and smile. They both spent the rest of the day with Megan and relaxed, feeling that the guilt had slowly elevated from their shoulders.

***

Susan's story, a testament to courage and resilience, wouldn't be forgotten. Her memory would continue to inspire him and countless others to fight for change, to break the silence surrounding sexual assault, and to ensure that no voice would ever go unheard. In the face of Brian's inevitable end, Eddie (Vance) knew that Susan's legacy would live on, a beacon of hope in a world that often felt shrouded in darkness.

Chapter 20

The sun dipped below the horizon, casting long shadows across Eddie (Vance)'s small apartment. He sat by the window, the dim light creating a soft halo around him, lost in the labyrinth of his thoughts. The weight of secrets and mistakes lay heavy on his shoulders, each one a ghost that haunted his waking moments and troubled his dreams.

He thought of Earl's death, a tragedy shrouded in silence and regret. The details of that fateful day were etched into his mind, a painful tableau of what-ifs and could-have-beens. The accident had been sudden, a cruel twist of fate that left Eddie (Vance) grappling with a profound sense of guilt. He had always blamed himself for causing the tragedy. The secret of Earl's death gnawed at him, a constant reminder of his perceived failure.

Then there was Susan, whose memory was a double-edged sword. Her final moments were seared into his heart, the pain and helplessness he felt as he held her hand while she took her last breath.

The promise he made to her had driven him to uncover the truth, but it also reminded him of the times he felt he had failed her in life. The knowledge of her suffering, the reality of her assault, and the monstrous truth about the man he had called his father had unraveled his world. The secrets surrounding Susan's trauma were a source of endless torment, and though he had fought for her justice, the guilt of not protecting her earlier lingered.

Hattie's presence in his life was another complex thread. Her absence had created a chasm in his family life, now filled with strained reunions and attempts to bridge years of separation. Their relationship had been tenuous, marked by distance and the unspoken pain of their shared past.

The secrets and mistakes tied to Hattie, Susan, and Earl, all being different yet equally burdensome, represented missed opportunities and the yearning for a bond that never fully solidified.

As Eddie (Vance) delved deeper into these reflections, the phone rang, pulling him back to the present. He glanced at the screen and saw Vance (Eddie)'s name. Vance (Eddie), a man with a story eerily similar to his own, had been a significant presence in Eddie (Vance)'s life.

Vance (Eddie)'s journey had its own shadows. He understood the unique pain of familial loss and the struggle to maintain relationships across the chasm life created.

"Hey, Vance," Eddie (Vance) answered, his voice tinged with the remnants of his somber reflection.

"Hey, Eddie," Vance (Eddie) replied, a note of warmth in his tone. "I was thinking about our conversation last week and wanted to see if you were up for a coffee. I found this new place that I think you'd like."

Eddie (Vance) hesitated, the weight of his thoughts pressing down on him. But Vance (Eddie)'s voice was a lifeline, a reminder that he wasn't alone in his struggles. "Sure, Vance. I'd like that. Where should we meet?"

Vance (Eddie) gave him the details, and soon Eddie (Vance) was heading out, his mind slowly shifting from the past to the present. The coffee shop Vance (Eddie) had found was a cozy, dimly lit place with an eclectic mix of furniture and a soothing atmosphere. Eddie (Vance) spotted Vance (Eddie) at a corner table, his face lighting up as he saw Vance approach.

"Glad you could make it," Vance (Eddie) said, standing to greet him with a firm handshake.

"Thanks for inviting me," Eddie (Vance) replied, a genuine smile breaking through his somber expression. They settled into their seats, the aroma of freshly brewed coffee filling the air.

As they sipped their drinks, their conversation flowed easily, each word a balm for their shared wounds. Eddie (Vance) found comfort in Vance (Eddie)'s understanding, in the knowledge that someone else had walked a similar path. As they talked, Eddie (Vance) felt a flicker of hope, a sense that maybe, just maybe, the secrets and mistakes of the past could be transformed into a foundation for a more connected future.

The coffee shop buzzed with the low hum of conversations and the clinking of cups and saucers. Eddie (Vance) and Vance (Eddie) sat in their corner, the intimate atmosphere providing a safe haven for the heavy truths that were about to be unveiled.

Eddie (Vance) took a deep breath, the weight of his secrets pressing heavily on his chest. He looked at Vance (Eddie), who had become more than just an acquaintance; he was a confidant, someone who understood the depths of his struggles.

"Vance, there's something I need to tell you," Eddie (Vance) began, his voice trembling slightly. "Something I've never shared with anyone."

Vance (Eddie) leaned forward, his expression serious and attentive. "Go on, Eddie. Whatever it is, I'm here for you."

Eddie (Vance)'s hands shook, and he clasped them together, his gaze dropping to the table. "Earl's death... he didn't fall down the stairs, I... I accidentally pushed him. We were arguing, and it got heated. I didn't mean for it to happen, but he lost his balance and fell."

The confession hung in the air between them, heavy and suffocating.

"It's alright, I won't tell a soul," Vance sighed and replied.

Relief washed over Eddie (Vance), the burden of his confessions slightly lifted by Vance (Eddie)'s promise. "Thank you, Vance. I can't tell you how much that means to me."

Vance (Eddie) nodded, his grip firm and steady. "We're in this together, Eddie. Family secrets can tear us apart, but they can also bring us closer if we handle them right."

Their conversation shifted back to lighter topics, but the bond between them had deepened, solidified by the shared weight of Eddie (Vance)'s confessions. As they finished their coffee and prepared to leave, Eddie (Vance) felt a strange mix of emotions – guilt, relief, and a glimmer of hope.

Outside the coffee shop, the city lights flickered like distant stars. Vance (Eddie) turned to Eddie (Vance), a serious expression on his face. "You know, Eddie, carrying these secrets is tough. But

I believe that confronting them and owning up to them is the first step towards healing. For both of us."

Eddie (Vance) nodded, the truth of Vance (Eddie)'s words sinking in. "You're right. And I need to start making amends, somehow. Not just for what happened with Earl and Hattie, but for everything."

Vance (Eddie) clapped him on the shoulder. "We'll figure it out together. One step at a time."

As Eddie (Vance) walked home, his mind replayed the evening's conversation. The secrets and mistakes of his past still weighed heavily on him, but sharing them with Vance (Eddie) had given him a new perspective. It wasn't about erasing the past but about finding a way to live with it, to learn from it, and to move forward.

The night air was cool and crisp, a refreshing contrast to the warmth of the coffee shop. Eddie (Vance) breathed deeply, feeling a small but significant shift within him. The road ahead would be challenging, but for the first time in a long while, he felt a sense of possibility.

He thought of Susan, her memory a guiding light in his darkest moments. He thought of Earl and the need to find some form of redemption for the accident that had claimed his life. And he thought of Hattie, and the complicated web of their relationship, knowing that the path to reconciliation would be long and difficult.

But with Vance (Eddie)'s support and the strength he found in his own resolve, Eddie (Vance) felt ready to face the future. He had made a promise to Susan, and he intended to keep it. Justice, truth, and healing – these were the pillars on which he would build the next chapter of his life.

As he reached his apartment, Eddie (Vance) looked up at the night sky, a sense of peace settling over him. The secrets of his past would always be a part of him, but they no longer defined him. He was ready to write a new story, one filled with hope, redemption, and the unwavering pursuit of justice.

***

Years had passed since the harrowing journey for justice began, and life had found a semblance of normalcy for Eddie (Vance). Despite the emotional and physical turmoil, he and Jennifer had managed to keep their marriage intact, bound by a deep love and mutual respect that had withstood the test of time.

Eddie (Vance) often reflected on the resilience of their relationship, especially during their evening walks through the park, a routine they had cherished since their early days together. The twilight would cast a gentle glow on Jennifer's face, and in those quiet moments, Eddie (Vance) felt a profound gratitude for the stability and warmth she brought into his life.

One evening, as they walked hand in hand, Eddie (Vance) broached a subject that had been on his mind. "Jennifer, do you ever think about how we've managed to stay together through everything?"

Jennifer smiled, her eyes crinkling at the corners. "All the time, Eddie. I think it's because we've always been honest with each other, even when it was hard. And because we've always chosen to face our challenges together rather than letting them pull us apart."

Eddie (Vance) squeezed her hand, the familiar comfort of her presence grounding him. "I couldn't have done it without you, you know. You've been my rock through everything – the investigation, the trial, the aftermath."

Jennifer stopped walking and turned to face him, her expression earnest. "And you've been mine, Eddie. We've both made sacrifices and carried burdens, but we've also lifted each other up. That's what a marriage is – a partnership. We've had our struggles, but we've always come back to each other."

As they continued their walk, Eddie (Vance) thought about the difficult times they had faced – the sleepless nights, the arguments, the moments of doubt. But through it all, their love had endured, growing stronger with each obstacle they overcame.

Back at home, they settled into their routine, preparing dinner together and sharing stories from their day. The kitchen, filled with the aroma of simmering spices and the sound of their laughter, was a sanctuary where they could momentarily escape the world's pressures.

Later, as they sat at the dinner table, Eddie (Vance) took a deep breath, feeling a sense of contentment wash over him. "Jennifer, I know I've said this before, but I need you to know how much I appreciate you. You've stood by me through the darkest times, and I don't take that for granted."

Jennifer reached across the table, her hand covering his. "And I appreciate you, Eddie. We've built a life together that's rich with love and shared experiences. I wouldn't trade that for anything."

Their marriage had been a journey marked by moments of profound joy and deep sorrow. They had celebrated triumphs and mourned losses, but through it all, their bond had remained unbroken. Eddie (Vance) knew that their love was not a fairy tale but a testament to their resilience and commitment to each other.

As the years went by, Eddie (Vance) and Jennifer continued to support each other in their individual pursuits. Eddie (Vance) remained dedicated to his advocacy work, helping survivors of sexual assault find their voices and fight for justice. Jennifer, too, found her own ways to contribute, volunteering at local shelters and offering her skills as a counselor to those in need.

Their shared mission of helping others became another thread that wove them closer together. They often collaborated on projects, combining their strengths and passions to make a difference in their community. Each success, no matter how small, was a shared victory that reinforced the strength of their partnership.

In their later years, Eddie (Vance)and Jennifer often reminisced about their journey, acknowledging the challenges they had faced and the love that had seen them through. Their home, filled with photographs and mementos of their life together, was a testament to their enduring bond.

One quiet evening, as they sat on the porch watching the sunset, Jennifer turned to Eddie (Vance) with a thoughtful expression. "You know, Eddie, we've had quite a life together. It's not always been easy, but it's been full of love and purpose."

Eddie (Vance) nodded, his heart full. "Yes, it has. And I'm grateful for every moment, Jennifer. We've built something beautiful together."

Jennifer smiled, her eyes shining with affection. "Here's to many more years, my love. Whatever the future holds, we'll face it together."

As the sun dipped below the horizon, casting a golden glow over their home, Eddie (Vance) felt a deep sense of peace. Their journey had been marked by trials and triumphs, but through it all, their love had remained a constant, unshakable force. And as they looked forward to the future, Eddie (Vance) knew that no matter what came their way, they would face it hand in hand, their hearts forever intertwined.

Made in the USA
Columbia, SC
07 April 2025